LOST PARADISE

Cees Nooteboom was born in the Hague in 1933. He is a poet and the author of prize-winning fiction and travel books. He won the Aristeion European Literature Prize for his novel *The Following Story*. His books have been translated into many languages.

D1637753

ALSO BY CEES NOOTEBOOM

Fiction

Rituals

Mokusei

A Song of Truth and Semblance

In the Dutch Mountains

Philip and the Others

The Knight Has Died

The Following Story

All Souls' Day

Non-Fiction

Roads to Santiago: Detours and Riddles in the Lands and History of Spain

Nomad's Hotel: Travels in Time and Space

CEES NOOTEBOOM

Lost Paradise

TRANSLATED FROM THE DUTCH BY
Susan Massotty

VINTAGE BOOKS
London

Published by Vintage 2008

2 4 6 8 10 9 7 5 3 1

Copyright © Cees Nooteboom 2004
English translation copyright © Susan Massotty 2007

Cees Nooteboom and Susan Massotty have asserted their rights
under the Copyright, Designs and Patents Act 1988
to be identified as the author and translator, respectively, of this work

This book is sold subject to the condition that it shall not,
by way of trade or otherwise, be lent, resold, hired out, or
otherwise circulated without the publisher's prior consent in any
form of binding or cover other than that in which it is published
and without a similar condition, including this condition, being
imposed on the subsequent purchaser

First published as *Paradijs Verloren* by Atlas in 2004
First published in Great Britain by Harvill Secker in 2007

Vintage
Random House, 20 Vauxhall Bridge Road,
London SW1V 2SA

www.vintage-books.co.uk

Addresses for companies within The Random House Group Limited
can be found at: www.randomhouse.co.uk/offices.htm

The Random House Group Limited Reg. No. 954009

A CIP catalogue record for this book
is available from the British Library

ISBN 9780099497158

Foundation for the
Production and
Translation of
Dutch Literature

The publishers gratefully acknowledge the support of the
Foundation for the Production and Translation of Dutch Literature

The Random House Group Limited supports The Forest
Stewardship Council (FSC), the leading international forest
certification organisation. All our titles that are printed on
Greenpeace approved FSC certified paper carry the FSC logo.
Our paper procurement policy can be found at
www.rbooks.co.uk/environment

Typeset by Palimpsest Book Production Limited,
Grangemouth, Stirlingshire

Printed and bound in Great Britain by
CPI Bookmarque, Croydon CR0 4TD

Any resemblance in this novel to living persons is pure chance, unless someone insists on recognising themselves or others, in which case they should be warned that fictional characters may be subject to a loss of reality. The Angel Project, however, did take place in Perth, Western Australia, in 2000, although that is not necessarily the year in which this story took place.

For Antje Ellermann Landshoff

A Klee painting named *Angelus Novus* shows an angel looking as though he is about to move away from something he is fixedly contemplating. His eyes are staring, his mouth is open, his wings are spread. This is how one pictures the angel of history. His face is turned toward the past. Where we perceive a chain of events, he sees one single catastrophe which keeps piling wreckage and hurls it in front of his feet. The angel would like to stay, awaken the dead, and make whole what has been smashed. But a storm is blowing in from Paradise; it has got caught in his wings with such a violence that the angel can no longer close them. The storm irresistibly propels him into the future to which his back is turned, while the pile of debris before him grows skyward. This storm is what we call progress.

Walter Benjamin, 'On the Concept of History'

PROLOGUE

'The pronoun *I* is better because more direct.'

From 'The Secretaries' Guide', in the section
'The Writer', *New Webster Encyclopedic Dictionary of the
English Language*, 1952

DASH 8-300. HEAVEN KNOWS, I'VE FLOWN IN ALL TYPES OF
aircraft, but this is the first time I have ever been in a Dash.
It's a small, compact plane, though it feels bigger because
there are very few passengers. The seat next to me is empty.
Apparently not many people are interested in flying from
Friedrichshafen to Berlin-Tempelhof. Our forlorn little
group of passengers walked from the no-frills terminal to
the plane – you can still do that here – and is now waiting
for take-off. The sun is shining, there is a stiff breeze. The
pilot, already up front, fiddles with the knobs. I hear the
co-pilot talking to the control tower. Empty moments like
these are familiar to anyone who does a lot of flying.

The engines have not been switched on yet. Some people have already started reading, others are staring out of the window, though there is not a great deal to see. I have taken out the in-flight magazine, but am not in the mood to do more than leaf through it: the usual airline propaganda, a few facts about the small number of cities this small company flies to — Bern, Vienna, Zurich — then a couple of freelance articles, one on Australia and the Aborigines, with pictures of rock drawings, brightly painted bark, all the latest trends. And another on São Paulo: a horizon lined with skyscrapers, the mansions of the rich and, of course, the ever so picturesque shanty towns — the slums or *favelas* or whatever you call the things. Corrugated-iron roofs, ramshackle wooden constructions, people who look as if they *like* living there. I have seen it all. I'd better not stare at the pictures too long, or they will make me feel a hundred years old. Maybe I *am* a hundred years old. All you have to do is multiply your real age by a magic number — a secret formula that includes every journey you have ever made and the unreal sense of déjà vu that goes with them — and you will find yourself in your dotage. I am not usually troubled by such thoughts, if only because they are hardly worth thinking about, but last night in Lindau I had three *Obstlers* too many, and at my age a strong schnapps like that takes its toll. The flight attendant looks outside, evidently expecting someone, and when she comes through the door, that someone turns out to be a woman — the kind of woman you hope will be seated next to you. Apparently I am not *that* old. But I am out of luck: she has been assigned a window seat in the row ahead of me, on the left-hand side of the plane. Actually, it is better this way, since now I can look at her as much as I want.

She has long legs in khaki trousers – a manly attribute that enhances her femininity – and her big, strong hands are trying to get at a book that has been carefully done up in crimson wrapping paper with Sellotape. Those big hands are impatient. When the tape does not immediately come off, she tears the parcel open. I am a voyeur. One of the great delights of travel is looking at people who do not know you are looking at them. She opens the book too rapidly for me to see the title.

I always want to know what people are reading, though in this case 'people' usually means 'women', since men no longer read. I have learned that women, whether they are on a train, on a park bench or at a beach, tend to hold their books in such a way that it is impossible to read the title. Look for yourself, and you will see what I mean.

I rarely summon up the nerve to ask them what they are reading, even when I am dying of curiosity. On the title page of this book, someone has written a long inscription. She scans it quickly, then puts the book on the empty seat beside her and stares out of the window. The engines are revving, which makes the small plane shake, and the sight of her breasts trembling gently in her tight-fitting T-shirt

3

is exciting. Her left knee is slightly raised. The light falls on her chestnut hair, giving it a golden sheen. The book is upside down, so I still cannot make out the title. It is a thin volume. I like that. Calvino says that books ought to be short, and for the most part he follows his own advice. The plane starts racing down the runway. Especially in smaller aircraft, there is always a sensual moment during take-off, when the plane finds a thermal and seems to get an extra lift, a kind of caress, similar to the feeling you had on swings when you were a child.

The hills are still covered in snow, which gives the landscape a very graphic feel: leafless trees etched on white paper. Sometimes that is all you need to convey an idea. She does not look at the view for long, but she picks up her book and reads the inscription again, as impatiently as the first time. I try to imagine what might have prompted the gift – that's my job, after all – but I don't get very far. A man trying to make amends for something? You've got to be careful with books. If you give someone the wrong book or the wrong writer, you will very soon find yourself in the doghouse.

She flicks through it, occasionally pausing to take a longer look at a particular page. For so short a book, it certainly has a lot of chapters. That means a new beginning each time, for which you ought to have a good reason. Any writer who botches the beginning or the end of a book has failed to grasp the basics, and the same goes for chapters.

Whoever the author of that book is, he has taken considerable risks. She has put down the book again, this time with the title right side up, but because of the glare from the overhead light, I cannot make out the words. I would have to stand to get a proper look.

'Cruising altitude.' I have always loved that expression. I expect to see skiers, since we are flying above clouds with glorious slopes. I never tire of looking at them. At this altitude the world has only blank pages, which you can fill in as you see fit. But she is not looking out of the window, she has picked up the in-flight magazine and has started reading it at the end. She races through São Paulo, lingers by a big green park, then stares at the Aboriginal paintings. From time to time she brings the magazine up close to her face, and once her long fingers even trace the strange figure of a serpent in one of the paintings. Then she closes the magazine and promptly falls asleep. Some people are able do that – sleep peacefully on a plane. She has one hand on her book and one behind her neck, beneath her reddish hair. The riddle that other people represent has occupied me all my life. I know there is a story here, and at the same time I know that I will never find out what it is. This book will remain closed, like the one on the seat. By the time we get ready for the landing at Tempelhof, a little over an hour later, I have written a quarter of an introduction to a book of photographs about cemetery angels. Below us are the anonymous high-rises of Berlin, along with the great historical fissure that still runs through the city. She combs her hair and picks up the wrapping paper. Before she rewraps the book, however, she smoothes the crimson paper across her thigh. I don't know why I find that so moving. Then, for a moment, she at last holds the book up high enough for me to read the two words of the title.

It's *this* book, a book out of which she is about to disappear, along with me. As I wait in the baggage-claim area, I see her walk rapidly through the exit doors, where there is a man waiting for her. She kisses him casually — as casually as she scanned the book, since the only part she actually read was the handwritten inscription that I did not read and did not write.

The bags arrive in no time. As I reach the upper level, she gets into a taxi with the man and then speeds away out of sight, leaving me, as always, behind with a few words. And with the city, which closes around me like a trap.

PART ONE

... *and from the other Hill*
To thir fixt Station, all in bright array
The Cherubim descended; on the ground
Gliding metéorous, as Ev'ning Mist
Ris'n from a River o're the marish glides,
And gathers ground fast at the Labourer's heel
Homeward returning. High in Front advanc't,
The brandisht Sword of God before them blaz'd
Fierce as a Comet; which with torrid heat,
And vapour as the Libyan Air *adust,*
Began to parch that temperate Clime; whereat
In either hand the hast'ning Angel caught
Our ling'ring Parents, and to th' Eastern Gate
Led them direct, and down the Cliff as fast
To the subjected Plaine; then disappeer'd.

Milton, *Paradise Lost*, Book XII

1

SOMEONE LEFT HER HOUSE IN JARDINS ONE HOT
summer evening while the smell of jacarandas and mag-
nolias filled the heavy, humid air. The Jardins district is
where the rich live, the people whose staff – cooks and
gardeners – have a long way to travel, two hours or more,
twice a day, to get to and from work. São Paulo is a big
city. When it rains, the buses are even slower than usual.

Someone left her house, borrowed her mother's second
car and went out for a drive with the music of Björk –
Nibelungen laments that seem out of place in the tropics
– turned up full blast. She sang along with the music, but
in a shrill, hysterical voice, working off a rage aimed at
no one in particular and a sadness that can be traced to no
particular source.

Someone drove down the Marginal, along the Tietê, past
the nouveau riche houses in Morumbi, and then, without
giving a thought to where she was going or what she was
doing, entered forbidden territory – not Ebú-Ecú, but
Paraisópolis, the very worst *favela* of all, a hell rather than

a paradise, and fraught with danger, making it, at that moment, irresistible. Someone was not doing the driving, the car was – the car and the music. Then all of a sudden the engine died, leaving only fear and Björk's high-pitched wails calling out to the wooden shacks, to the smells, to the moonlight on the corrugated-iron roofs, and to the noises coming from the cheap TVs, shouting in reply and mingling with the sounds of excited laughter, of voices coming closer and closer until they formed a circle around her and would not let her go. After that everything happened fast, too fast for her to panic or shout or run away. She no longer remembers how many of them there were, but she will always blame herself, even more than for driving into the *favela*, for the disgustingly poetic falsification she came up with afterwards out of sheer self-preservation: that it had been like a black cloud. She had been enveloped by a black cloud. And then she had screamed, of course, it had hurt, of course, but as her clothes were being ripped off, there had been laughter, unforgettable laughter, strident and ecstatic, a sound next to the sound welling up out of a world that had never existed for her before, a hate and a rage so deep that they could swallow you up forever, and yet just as that hysterical shriek rang out, panting voices had urged each other on – something she would remember as long as she lived. They had not bothered to kill her, but had simply left her behind as if she were rubbish. Perhaps that had been the worst thing, the way the voices had disappeared again, back into their own lives, in which she had been a mere incident. Later the police asked her what she had been doing in that area, and obviously she knew that what they were really saying was that it had all been her fault, when in fact the thing she did actually blame herself for was that humiliating lie about the cloud, because clouds don't rip your clothes off, men do. It is men who force their way into your body and into your life, leaving behind a puzzle that you will never be able to solve. Or rather that *I* will never be able to solve, since that someone was me, the same me who is now on the other side of the world, lying beside a man who is as dark as they were, a man who has taken nothing of mine, who is a mystery to me and will soon go away again. I am not sure whether my being here is a good thing, though why wouldn't it be? Because he doesn't know why I'm here. Not the *real* reason anyway. And he is never going to find out. In that sense I am deceiving him.

I am here to exorcise a demon; he is here to have sex with me. Or so I assume. In any case that is what we have done. A week, he said, not longer. Then he has to go back to his mob. His mob, his clan – that is how they refer to it here. But he hasn't told me where his mob is. Somewhere in the outback, somewhere in this country's endless space. I have no idea what is going through his mind. Maybe he is also deceiving me. Can someone lie who scarcely says a word?

He is asleep, and when he's asleep, he is time itself. These are the oldest people on earth, and they have lived in this country for at least forty thousand years. You can't get any closer to eternity than that. I went for a drive one night in São Paulo and ended up here. Not exactly, but that is how I think of it. I shouldn't be thinking such things, but no one can forbid me to think them. I stare at the man asleep beside me. As young as he is, he looks as though he has lived a thousand years. He is lying on the ground, curled up like an animal. When he opens his eyes, he is as old as the rocks, as old as the lizards you see in the desert, although he wears his age lightly because he moves lightly, as if he cannot feel the weight of his body. I tell myself that this is as big a lie as the other one, but that's not true. I have become involved in something I have no control over, because my time here does not count. Every once in a while, when he and I are out in the desert – in a country that consists almost entirely of desert – when he points out things that I have failed to see, when he all but becomes the land itself and knows where to find water in places I would never be able to find it, when I feel humbled in the face of his immeasurable age, which allows him to see food where I see sand, then I think – against my better judgement – that I left my house that night in order to arrive at this place. I left the heaviness of the tropics, where all is motion and noise, to arrive at this stillness.

2

I WOULD NEVER HAVE COME HERE BUT FOR ALMUT.
Almut's grandfather is German, as mine is. Ever since we
started school, we have been known collectively as Almut
and Alma. We laugh at the funny accents of our grand-
fathers, who came to Brazil after the war and never want
to talk about their pasts. Even though they are constantly
homesick, they have never been back to the *Heimat*. They
weep and wail along with Fischer-Dieskau and the
Kindertotenlieder. They want Germany to win the World Cup.
But they don't want to talk about the war, just as our fathers
don't want to talk about their fathers. Our fathers didn't
want to learn German either. Almut and I would like to,
but it's a beastly language. Everything is the very opposite
of Portuguese: masculine nouns are feminine and vice versa.
Death is masculine, the sun is feminine, and yet the moon
is masculine – there is no rhyme or reason to it. A beastly
language to learn, I mean, not to listen to, except when
they shout. Almut is tall and blonde, so all Brazilians fall
for her. I come up to her shoulder, and always have, even

when we were kids. 'I like it that way,' Almut said. 'I can easily put my arm around your shoulder.' I thought she was prettier, but she thought she was too big. 'I'm a Germanic ur-mother,' she always said. 'They should have called me Brunhilde. Now, look at those breasts. Whenever I walk down the street, I immediately have half a samba school following me. You don't have that problem. That's because of the shadow.' The 'shadow' was one of her pet theories. 'There's a shadow inside you.' 'How can you tell?' 'I can see it in your eyes, beneath your eyes, on your skin, everywhere.' 'But what is it?' 'It's your secret.' I looked in the mirror that night and didn't see a thing. Or rather, only my face. I'm not sure I have a secret. 'That doesn't matter,' Almut said. 'You *are* a secret, even if you don't realise it. No one ever knows what you're thinking. When you say something, the words don't seem to match the expression on your face. It's as though you're holding something back, a kind of "Trespassers Beware". It's bound to get you into trouble one day, but don't let it frighten you.'

I don't remember how old we were when we had this conversation – probably about fifteen – but I have never forgotten it. Another thing she said to me was, 'It's as if you're not alone, as if you always have someone with you.' Almut and I did everything together, to the despair of our first boyfriends. We spent hours lying in the hammock on the porch, discussing our future. We were going to study art history – that had been decided already. Modern art for her, the Renaissance for me. 'All those Crucifixions and Annunciations make me sick,' she would say. We never agreed on this point. I could do without the Crucifixions, though it was fascinating to see how various artists dealt with the same subject, but it was the Annunciations that I adored. I have this thing about angels. Raphael, Botticelli, Giotto — as long as there are wings. 'That's because you wish *you* could fly,' Almut says.

'Don't you?' 'No, not me.' Her walls were lined with Willem de Kooning and Dubuffet and all those disintegrating figures and faces of the cubists that I disliked. Mine were lined with angels. Almut referred to it as my 'aviary'. 'What I hate about angels,' she often said, 'is that you can't tell if they're male or female.'

'They're male.'

'How do you know?'

'They have male names: Michael, Gabriel . . .'

'It would have been much more logical for a woman to have come and told Mary she was going to have a baby.'

'Women fly differently.'

Which was absurd, since I had never seen a woman fly, but you know you are right about some things. Giotto, for example, got the idea for his swooping angels from seeing a comet. His angels fly through the air so fast that their feet are swallowed up in a trail of light. A woman would never fly like that.

'Every so often I dream that I'm flying,' Almut said. 'I

go very slowly, so you may be right. How do you think angels land?'

I remember that moment with perfect clarity. We were in the Uffizi in Florence, looking at my favourite painting: Botticelli's 'Annunciation'. Almut had just finished saying that she had had enough of creatures with wings.

'You've dragged me all over Europe to look at angels. Why don't you put yourself in Mary's place? There you are, sitting peacefully in your room, knowing nothing of what is about to happen, and suddenly you hear the flapping of wings, as if a giant bird is going to land. Have you ever wondered what it must have sounded like? You can hear the wing-beat of a dove, so imagine the flapping of wings a hundred times bigger. The noise must have been deafening: "Crew, prepare for landing."'

But I didn't want to listen to her chatter. I have always been able to tune people out. The moment something touches my inner self – my secret, as Almut would call it – I retreat into my own world. I know other people are out there, but no matter who they are, they no longer exist for me.

'There's something creepy about it,' Almut once said. 'You're no longer there. And I know you're not bluffing.'

'It's concentration.'

'No, it's more than that. It's absence. I might as well not be here. I used to feel insulted. There was something contemptuous about it. It was as if *I* didn't exist any more, while all along it was *you* who didn't.'

I tuned her out. The first sight of a painting that you know only from reproductions is a kind of hallucination. You can't believe you are actually looking at the real thing, that hundreds of years ago Botticelli stood before this very picture – staring at it with eyes long since turned to dust – and applied the finishing touches. I can feel his presence, hovering in the vicinity of the painting, but he is unable to get close to it. So much time has gone by that the painting has become something completely different, and yet it is the same physical object, and that is what makes it so scary. The original painting has a magical effect on me, producing an indescribable dizziness. If I also had to listen to the people going past the painting, giving it a quick glance and walking on, I would faint. I went to a *candomblé* session in Bahia once. The woman who was dancing was in a world of her own. If someone had shocked her out of her trance right then, she would have fallen in a heap. That is more or less how I feel.

Quiet hysteria. Another one of Almut's observations. Said with a smile, but still . . .

Meanwhile, I have become wholly absorbed by the painting. Red rectangular floor tiles, a regular pattern whose straight lines contrast with the swirling motion and the pleats and folds in the clothing of the two figures for whom the rest of the world does not exist either. All is calm: the angel has just arrived. He kneels on one knee, his right hand reaching up towards the woman standing over him, who bends towards him. Their hands are almost touching, a gesture of electrifying intimacy. Both figures have their fingers spread wide, as if this is the language in which they wish to express themselves, since no words have yet been uttered. The woman looks away, otherwise she would see the fear in the angel's deference. Few people, I believe, ever think about the inherent absurdity. A winged man flies into the room – his wings are still slightly outspread – and while that one tall spindly tree rises from the serene landscape in the Mediterranean light beyond the window, he bears a message from a world millions of miles away and yet so near, a world that knows neither time nor distance, a world that is now nestled inside the woman. I don't know what divinity is. Or rather, I don't know how to describe it. How do people bear the touch of the divine? I don't think such a thing is possible. But if it is, it must look very much as it does in this painting.

'You don't believe in all that rigmarole, do you?' Almut was bound to ask me that.

'No, except that in the painting every bit of it is true. That's what it's all about.'

Just then the angelus rang, which was of course also what it was all about. *Angelus Domini nuntiavit Mariae*. Some stories are powerful enough, even after two thousand years, even in the age of computers, to make a bell ring. And Botticelli knew that.

An hour later, as we were standing on the Ponte Vecchio,

looking down at the swiftly flowing waters of the Arno, Almut said, 'Try to imagine it.'

'Imagine what?'

'Making love to an angel. The wings must be a bonus – all that rustling and flapping when he comes. Or when he spreads his wings and flies off with you. The closest I ever got to it was with an airline pilot, and that was a total flop.'

'The only angel you'd ever fall for is the one in the El Greco painting in Toledo, the guy with the scraggly wings who looks as if he's being dragged into heaven.'

'The one with the turned-up nose? Oh, thanks. Though he does radiate a lot of power.'

I can count on Almut to bring me back down to earth.

3

I COUNTED ON HER THEN TOO. ALMUT DEALT WITH everything, coming down to the police station and taking me to a gynaecologist. I don't know which was more humiliating: the uniformed policemen who kept asking me what I was doing in the *favela*, making me repeat the story over and over so they could get off on it themselves, or the chromium table with those awful stirrups and the mumbling head down between my legs, looking for traces of semen – or even worse – and finally observing that I had got off lightly, though for all I knew he doubted anything had happened. The only person who was allowed to ask me why I had driven there that night was Almut.

'Was it the mood?'

Mood. Just a word, an ordinary word. Almut once told me that it comes from the Old Saxon *mod*, but I didn't like the sound and have never wanted to look it up. Sometimes I would sooner ask a question than know the answer. Anyway, it was a code word between us; we both knew exactly what it meant. One day, when I was twelve or thirteen, I tried to explain to her how it feels – the terrifying fear that sucks me into a bottomless pit, as if I am about to tumble off the edge of the world. It is hard to put into words. You are dragged out to sea, incapable of resisting the pull, or actually not wanting to, since your one desire is to disappear forever, to be consumed by the menacing darkness, to seek out your fear so that you can surrender yourself to it, yet while all of this is going on you feel dizzy and you hate your disgustingly dizzy body – all you want is to be rid of it, to make it go away, to make the thinking stop. Rage, pleasure, melancholy are all rolled into one, and when it's over, I'm left with a terrible sharpness – a white, electrifying clarity – in which I realise that I don't want to be alive, that everything is riddled with hate – plants, ordinary objects, the road I take to school every day – until that too subsides, leaving behind a sensual composure, in which I feel reconciled to the world again, though at the same time I know that the whole thing is paper-thin, transparent, an illusion, that I will never be able to make my peace with the world because I am part of it and yet not part of it – a contradiction I need to resolve. 'You've got that look again,' Almut would say at such moments. 'Come on, let's exorcise the demons.' And then in her room or mine we would dance like mad to the music of Chico Buarque or the Stones or whoever, until we collapsed on the floor and lay side by side. From there we would set off on our great journey. Almut had an enormous map of the world taped to the ceiling. I can still see it. It wasn't like most maps: Siberia and Alaska, looking strangely elongated, were not at the top of the map, but on the left and right sides; Australia had been moved to the top, making it look even more like an island, an island hovering above the rest of the world, and we knew we would go there one day, to that upside-down world where everything was different, where the whites were the descendants of convicts and felons who had clung to the edges of this huge island because the land in between was a broiling-hot desert inhabited by the others – the people who had lived there forever and looked as if they had sprung from the land itself: scorched, sun-seared beings who trod softly over the earth and lived as if time didn't exist; they, too, lived an upside-down life unlike that of anyone else on the planet, as if all they had ever wanted was simply to be, and had passed down this changeless existence without ever changing anything in the world. We read about the Dreamtime, the time before time and memory began, when the world was flat and empty and shapeless and there were no trees or animals or food or people, until at a certain moment the Heroes, their mythical ancestors, appeared. No one knows quite how it happened, whether they came out of the ocean or the air or over the edge of the world. *Os heróis creativos* – in my language the words resound with an enchantment that still fills me with awe whenever I say them. Almut and I knew exactly what we meant when either of us spoke those words, for they invariably triggered our dreams and imaginings. We knew the country so well you would have thought we had been there a hundred times: Cairns, Alice Springs, Coral Bay, Kalgoorlie, Broome, Derby. One day we would go to Australia and travel through the desert from Meekatharra to Wiluna, and from Wiluna to Mungilli. We would criss-cross the country, see Ayers Rock and Arnhem Land and the Nullarbor Plain, which looked like Mars. Australia was our secret. We collected everything we could lay our hands on: back issues of *National Geographic*, brochures from travel agencies, everything. Almut had hung up a print of some-thing called the Sickness Dreaming Place: spirits, swaying white figures drawn on a cliff, surrounded by lines the colour of dried blood, lines that also ran through their bodies, which were divided into odd geometrical planes. They had no mouths, and red holes where their eyes should have been, and fan-shaped things above their heads. I don't know how long we went on fantasising, but even now I can feel the intensity of our dreams. Sitting beneath Almut's print, which I can picture clearly even now, we discussed everything of interest to us: boyfriends, quarrels at home, bad school reports, all of which melted away in the face of those swaying, healing spirits, who had become *our* spirits – patron saints we would one day visit, when we really needed them.

4

LOOKING BACK ON IT, I THINK THAT WHAT APPEALED TO us was that they never wrote anything down. There were no written records. All kinds of things were sacred, but nothing had been preserved in a book. Nor had they invented any machines, a fact for which they are often ridiculed, and yet they have survived for tens of thousands of years in a hostile environment, a kind of eternity without numbers, in which they had managed to live off the land without destroying it. There was no point in longing for a return to this way of life, because our world had been the death of theirs. The only visible clue to what they had been thinking during this eternity was their art, and even that was not intended to be permanent: sand drawings, body paintings applied during ritual ceremonies, art that belonged to everyone, except to us, because we did not have the keys to their secrets. All we could hope to do was scratch the surface. We wanted to understand it, but we couldn't. It was at once an abstraction and a physical reality. How could that be translated into something you could understand?

The Dreaming that had nothing to do with dreaming, but was a noun used to express an entire world order, from the origin of the universe to the time before memory began. It was too much for our seventeen-year-old brains to grasp, and to be honest, it still is. The lightning men, the rainbow snake, and all those other beings in human and non-human forms who created everything as they travelled through the chaos of the unformed world and taught people how to deal with the universe — it was all that and more. During the Dreamtime, their mythical ancestors had cast a net of Dreamings over the world. Sometimes a Dreaming belonged only to the people who lived in a certain place, but when they trekked across the desert, that same Dreaming linked them to people in other areas, even though they might speak a different language. This could be seen in the landscape — the spirits and ancestors had left tracks everywhere in the form of stones, water pools or rock formations, so that future generations could read the stories and thus relive their own history. But that was not all. Not only did the Dreamings make it possible for people to see and recognise the still-active powers of those ancestral beings in the landscape, but each person had his own set of Dreamings that linked him to his ancestors. All of this was expressed by means of what we now call art. You used it to express your own spiritual identity, your totem, which was linked to an animal or a physical feature of the landscape, to songs no one else was allowed to sing, to dances and secret signs — a cosmogony in which there were no written-down rules, but in which everything — literally — had its place, to which you or your group always returned, a world without a written language, but with a permanent encyclopedia of signs, still legible after tens of thousands of years, which would guide you to your rightful place. The more Almut and I read, the less we understood. It was too much and too complex, and yet it was its visibility that drew us back again and again and gradually gave us the feeling that we might be able to leave our own world. This was our secret, which we did not have to share with anyone else. One of our favourite photographs was of an old man painting the side of a cliff. He was sitting with his left leg tucked under him. You could tell by his frizzy white hair that he was old, though his body still looked young. It gleamed — all except his feet, that is, which were ashen and leathery, the feet of a man who had never worn shoes and who would soon walk away and leave his painting behind, someone whose way of thinking was very different from ours, who believed that the Creative Heroes had emerged into an empty world, that they could appear in the shape either of animals or of people, that they could change each other into rocks or trees or hurl each other into the air to create the moon or the planets. We never doubted for a moment that we would go there one day, and even after Almut and I went to Europe — Dresden, Amsterdam and Florence — as part of our art history studies, Australia kept calling and beckoning to us. At the mere mention of the place, we would look at each other with the conspiratorial smile of two people who shared a secret that no one would ever be able to take from us. After what happened in the *favela*, I didn't leave the house for weeks. I had no wish to see anyone and couldn't talk to my parents about it. Almut came to the house from time to time and sat by my bed. She knew there was no need for words, until the day she told me she had been looking into cheap flights to Australia. We could fly to Sydney. From there we could go to Arnhem Land and El Shirana, which was not far from Sleisbeck. We could go to the Sickness Dreaming Place. She did not need to elaborate. We both knew what she meant by that.

5

ALMUT HAS TWO PARENTS OF GERMAN DESCENT. I HAVE a fair amount of Latin blood flowing through my veins. My father is a real Teuton (you could put him in a uniform and he would feel right at home), but at least he had the good sense to marry my mother. If he is Wagner, she is Verdi – with a vengeance. This is never more obvious than when they are having an argument. 'He only picked me because he was curious,' my mother always said. 'He never knew who he was having to deal with – the Portuguese, Jewish, Indian or Italian in me. He wanted to see which one had the upper hand. But he underestimated the Indians.' They are still a mystery to him. To me too. The shadow, the mood – that's the Indian in me. My mother has it too. We have learned to stay out of each other's way when we get it.

Almut has banished chaos from her life. She is Germanic and has a feeling for order. She is the one who, years ago, came up with our Australia piggy bank. And she is also the one who said, also years ago, that we should acquire a skill that would enable us to earn money when we were travelling, so we would not forever end up washing dishes in restaurants or bars, or babysitting, or worse. As a result, we took a course in physical therapy: exercises for people with back problems, massage, that kind of thing.

'It'll be useful all over the world,' Almut said.

'In sex joints, you mean.'

'Why not? As long as they keep their filthy hands off me!'

6

'I'M ONLY LENDING HIM TO YOU,' THE GALLERY OWNER in Adelaide had said, as if he were talking about a book or a painting. An object. The artist either had not heard it or had pretended not to — the latter, I think.

There was an exhibition of Aboriginal painters from all over Australia. His painting was black — a night sky studded with infinitesimally small white dots, though even the word 'dot' makes them sound too big. Your first thought, of course, was that they were stars, but that would have been too easy. At first you saw only a monochrome black canvas. Only later did you notice the thousands of minuscule points that may or may not have been stars. Through the intricate net of dots you could vaguely make out an even darker shape: the Dreaming of a totem animal, which in turn represented the flow of a tiny stream — so abstract that eyes such as ours cannot even see it. Of course it has nothing to do with our eyes. The problem is that we keep encountering a different mindset. He tried to explain it to me, but had little success. He did not look at me the whole time he was talking to me. Every word seemed to require a tremendous effort. Although Almut and I had read up on the subject earlier, it now appeared that we had simply been reading stories that could never be as real to us, as natural, as that painting was to him. The painting itself was not the problem. You could find the same kind of thing in any museum in the United States or Brazil, *Desert Lizard Dreaming at Night*. Why not? Nor was it the fact that I could not make out a desert lizard. Dreaming — there was that word again. You could not avoid it and you could not get around it. It was a word you kept tripping over, again and again. It seemed to make sense in English, but try saying it in another language and have it mean the same thing: a religion, a sacred era, the time of the mythical ancestors, as well as laws, ritual, ceremony, the state of mind in which the paintings had been made, because in this case he had inherited his Dreaming — that of the desert lizard — from his father and grandfather. How could you inherit something that wasn't a physical object? Somewhere inside him, in his genealogical make-up, his inner being, there was an invisible lizard that was not in fact a lizard and would never be visible to me in his paintings, and yet it was one of his ancestors, in the guise of an animal, who had come to him out of unmeasured time and had kept its sacred meaning even after the arrival of the others, who knew nothing of their traditions and way of life and did their best to undermine and overpower it. Dreaming. I liked to say the word

33

to myself, as if that might enable me to participate in their spiritual kingdom, in the spirit-filled realm of these paintings, which otherwise seemed to survive only on reserves, far away in the merciless desert that some of them could still read like a book or a song. Everyone had his own Dreaming, which came with a set of totems and songs that made up his own personal lineage and were a legacy from the still continuing act of creation performed by his ancestors, which is also known as the Dreaming. None of this could be seen in the cities any more. Most white Australians seemed to struggle with these metaphysical concepts, if only because the Aborigines they came into contact with were like human driftwood – people who had lost their ancestral ties and therefore no longer belonged anywhere. Australians like these had little use for the concept of sacred sites, of ground that no human being should be allowed to tread, especially when gold or silver or other coveted commodities lay beneath that ground.

7

THIS IS NOT GOING TO HELP ME AT ALL. THE SILENCE of the great outdoors here is like nothing else on earth, as are the starry skies. A desert stillness, a desert sky. In the faint light of a carbide lamp I can see his skin, which is of the same matt blackness as his painting and has the same white luminosity, as though an infinitely far-off Milky Way is hidden beneath the black. He can breathe without making a sound. Nothing makes a sound here. If only I myself could be more quiet, I am sure I would be able to hear the shifting grains of sand, the slithering of the desert lizard and the wind in the spinifex and the balgas — the grass trees. Assuming there is a bit of wind, which tonight there isn't. I have travelled a long way and have arrived here. I am trying to put my thoughts into words, but I cannot. I am getting nowhere. I would like to say something about my body, about how I have realised, more than ever, that it will be there only once, that it coincides with what I call 'me', but I reach a point where things can no longer be described in words. One cannot talk about ecstasy. And yet that is what I mean. I have never existed as much. It has nothing to do with him. Or rather, he is only part of it. He belongs to all of those things out there, in a way in which I have never belonged to my surroundings, though everything is different: I am the equal of all of those things. I can't think of a better way to express it. I wouldn't dare say that to anyone but Almut, and I am not even ready to do that. I know she wouldn't laugh at me – I have always been able to tell her everything – but now is not the right time. 'I am the equal of the stillness, the sand, the starry sky.' You can't tell anyone that. Nor can you say, 'I'm just one small person, but for the first time in my life I finally know where my place is. Nothing else can happen to me.' No, you definitely can't say that. It's another one of those things you would rather not say, even though it is how you feel. I am not hysterical, I know what I am saying. I also know that Almut understands me. Though our relationship will be short, this man has helped me catch up with my shadow, and that is good. We are one now; I am both dark and light. If I were to get up and go outside, I know I would not see a light anywhere. I stood out there last night, and there were only two things in the universe – me, and all of those other things, in which case it no longer matters that I will disappear from it one day, because I have seen and understood everything. I have become inaccessible, I feel above it all. If I were an instrument, I would produce the most beautiful music. I know you can't say any of this to another

36

living soul, but it is true. For the first time in my life I understand what they meant in the Middle Ages by the 'harmony of the spheres'. When I stand outside here, I do not just *see* the stars, I *hear* them.

Who banned angels from our thoughts? I can feel them all around me. My Master's thesis was on the portrayal of musical angels: Hieronymus Bosch, Matteo di Giovanni, and especially one particular illustration in a fourteenth-century illuminated manuscript. It shows St Denis at his writing desk, working on his book about the hierarchy of the angels. Arrayed in nine arcs above his mitred head are angels carrying medieval musical instruments. They fly towards each other with their violins and horns, their psalteries and tambourines, their organs and cymbals. As I lie here in the desert, I listen to their music: an incredible jubilation amid the silence. Angels, desert lizard, rainbow snake, the heroes of creation – everything at last comes together. I have arrived. And when I leave, I will not need to take anything with me. I have everything.

8

I THINK ABOUT WHAT I HAVE BEEN SAYING. NONE OF
those words – psalteries, mitred, angels, cymbals – are part
of his vocabulary. At least that's what I thought, but he
laughed at me.

No, that's not the right expression. He laughed me off,
pushing me back with a faraway look in his eyes. This will
be the shortest affair I have ever had, and I will remember
every moment as if it lasted an eternity. He is spoiling me
for every other man, but I don't care. He came into my life
at just the right time. There is a lot I don't understand. You
can see right through our faces, but not through his. His
face might as well be made of onyx – it reveals nothing.
Where does he come from? He showed me a map of
Australia. It had the same familiar shape – a kind of sleeping
ox without a head – but instead of the usual boundaries,
there were coloured areas with the names of indigenous
peoples – Ngaanyatjarra, Wawula, Pitjantjatjara – who have
become extinct or might even still be alive, for all I know.
Each name represents a language, living or dead. 'They

ought to abolish the word "Aboriginals",' he said, but he didn't tell me where he came from. He doesn't want to talk about any of the concepts that brought me here: the myths, the Dreamtime, the dream creatures, his own ancestry. In the gallery's prospectus on his work, there was a story about his totem, the desert lizard, but when I asked him about it, he shrugged.

'Don't you believe in any of that any more?' I asked.

'If I still believed in it, I wouldn't be allowed to talk about it.'

'So you don't believe in it any more?'

'It's not that simple.'

End of conversation.

I try to achieve a cool objectivity, to see it all through someone else's eyes: who I am, my personal story, how I came to be here, my dreams of an Australia that has turned out to be so very different from what I had expected, the months I have spent in this country. I wonder if I have been lying to myself, but I haven't. I'm not crazy – if this is ecstasy, it is of the highest order, something I have longed for, something that does not necessarily have to last. On the contrary, the fact that it will not last is a prerequisite. Maybe it's against some kind of law for someone to look at you, put his hands on your shoulders, tell you he can stay for just one week, then up and leave. It is as if you are forced to cram a whole life into one week. Inconceivable.

9

MY AUSTRALIA WAS A FICTION, AN ESCAPE, WHICH I realised the moment the plane touched down. I was completely dehydrated after the long flight, and was feeling apprehensive. Almut had slept the whole time, most of it with her heavy head on my shoulder, but when eventually she woke up, she tugged at my arm, urging me to look at Orion, hanging a bit crookedly in the Australian sky, as if the Hunter had taken a fall. I could feel her trembling with excitement. We have always been different in that respect. I shrink in the face of change, and she expands. She was bubbling over, a very physical reaction, as if she couldn't wait for the plane to land, wanted to fly on ahead and drag me with her.

Not even the terminal could dampen her spirits. She did not seem to notice the smell that permeates most airports and could not possibly usher in the Dreamland we had imagined all those years ago in our rooms in São Paulo. This was the land of the conquerors. I heard them speaking in their loud twangy voices in the language that had stamped out all those other languages, and realised that I had made a fatal mistake, a feeling that wore off only after a couple of days. Almut's reaction was the very opposite. She arrived in a state of euphoria that lasted for weeks. We found a kind of hippy hotel, where we could do our own cooking. We did not have work permits, but that was not a problem. In the first week Almut found a job with a so-called physical therapist, though she warned me not to expect too much. 'I'm only there for the placebo effect. We get a lot of little old ladies with arthritis, and windsurfers who have been taken apart. God, those guys are big! What bodies! Endless, and you can't skip a single muscle. I've never seen so much meat! If you took a bite out of that, your cholesterol would soar sky high. And they've got a sex drive to match – it goes into high gear the minute they walk through the door. But I won't even start down that road.'

A few weeks later she did go down that road and got fired.
    'How could you be so stupid?'
    She shrugged. 'I'm Brazilian. Not that it's in my genes, but it must have rubbed off somehow. Besides, they're so sweet. They don't know what to do with those enormous bodies of theirs. They're goddam buildings. Now I understand where the term "bodybuilder" comes from. They can surf, play rugby, race across the desert, hoist half a buffalo on to a barbecue spit, but beyond that? They've got *poco* sophistication. Not the ones that I met anyway. Besides, the guy was so tall it took my breath away. He wasn't just a man, he was a walking

phallic symbol! You could put him in a temple of Shiva, and the whole village would bring him offerings. And then those big blue Mummy-help-me eyes, with a jungle cry thrown in for free. I nearly had a heart attack. But then my boss came charging in and that was that.'

Almut pursed those narrow Puritan lips. Queen Victoria to the life! 'God, what an English bitch. "Miss Kopp! This is a *decent* establishment!" Oh well, at least I've got another one for my diary. But what are we going to do now?'

It was raining. I had a job at a beach café, but they had called to say I didn't have to come in. That was the deal. No sun, no work. No work, no pay. Fair enough.

'Do you remember why we came here?' Almut asked me.

I did. We had come here to go to the Sickness Dreaming Place, though neither of us had ever spoken of it again. Nor of our other reason. After all, you could hardly admit, even to each other, that you had come to Australia to see Aborigines.

Almut, guessing my thoughts, said, 'Do you remember how we imagined this country? How we were hoping to find the Dreamtime? I haven't met anyone who even remotely resembles the people we used to dream about. They simply are not there. At any rate, I haven't come across them. All I've seen are a couple of lost souls in a park.'

'That's hardly a news item. You knew that before you came.'

'Yes, but not that it would look like this. Like a concen-

42

tration camp without the fences. You can smell the beer a mile off.'

'You sound like an Australian. I've heard them say that a thousand times . . . There are two Aborigines at the place where I work.'

'Sure, in the kitchen. Washing dishes and carrying out the rubbish.'

'They're nice guys.'

'I'm sure they are. Have you talked to them? Have you asked them where they're from?'

But I hadn't talked to them. Or rather, they hadn't talked to me.

The thing that struck me most was the way they walked, though it is hard to describe. 'Lopsided' is not the right word, but something like that. They glided across the room on long thin legs with knobbly knees. They somehow walked as if they were not really there. The fact that they did not look at you only made it worse. I don't know if 'shy' is the right word, but we never had an actual conversation. The rest of the staff made no effort either. Once, when I brought it up with one of the cooks, a student, he said, 'You're reading too much into it. You foreigners always have big expectations. Half of what you read is false. Their world has ceased to exist. The ones you see here have fallen between the cracks. They'll have to pull themselves out on their own. All those stories you hear about sacred sites are beautiful, of course, but what can you do? I admit that what happened to them is terrible, but I repeat: what can you do? Or rather, what can *they* do? Paint their bodies for your entertainment? Pretend we never came here? They lost. That might be disgraceful, but what are we supposed to do? Pay reparations, make detours around their sacred sites even when there's uranium underneath? This is the twenty-first century. Wait until you go to one of those reserves. They put on quite a show, a kind of living museum. You get to travel back in time — for a fee. If they let you in, that is. It may sound crazy, but the ones I respect the most are the ones who say "keep out" and "piss off", and then go on broiling in their sandbox a thousand miles from nowhere, pretending the world outside doesn't exist, as they have for thousands of years. Except that in those days our world really didn't exist.'

'Theirs did,' I said.

'You don't have to convince *me*. But they're living in a bell jar. You don't have a solution, neither do I, and neither do any of those do-gooders, who'd like nothing better than to preserve them all in a freezer forever. And then you have the ones who make money out of them: the museum curators, the gallery owners, the anthropologists. No, you can't turn back the clock.'

'A penny for your thoughts,' Almut said. 'Do you even remember the question?'

'You asked me what we should do next.'

'That's not so strange, is it? Look around you. Is this the House of Anglo-Saxon Sorrow, or what? I want to hear a *bem-te-vi*, I want to hear a *periquito*, I want to hear a *sabiá*, I want to see an *ipe roxo*, I want to see the purple blossoms of a *quaresmeira*, I want to eat a *churrasco* at Rodeio, I want to drink an ice-cold beer at Frevo, I want to buy a bikini at Bazar 13, I want to watch my grandfather play cards at the Hipica Paulista . . .'

'You're homesick.'

'Maybe.'

'But what about the Sickness Dreaming Place?'

'Bingo. Tomorrow.'

'How are we going to get there?'

'We'll fly to Alice Springs, buy a 4x4, some old clunker, and drive up north to Darwin. That'll put us right back in the tropics.'

'And my job?'

'Quit it. We'll find something else. I hate this brown couch, I hate that picture of that creepy-little-girl-and-her-pony-on-her-first-day-at-school, I hate these wobbly plastic chairs and I hate that stupid cow with the spots on her face. "Could you please cook normal food, darling? The whole house smells like an African village . . ."'

'Right, let's go. First the travel agent. Then Arnhem Land.'

10

ALICE SPRINGS. IT HAS ONLY BEEN A FEW WEEKS, BUT AS
Almut says, 'All past time is present time.' The central busi-
ness district is a grid of streets between Wills Terrace and
Stuart Terrace, eight blocks bordering on a river that isn't
a river. The Todd River shown on the map is in reality an
ochre-coloured sandpit with a few thirsty-looking trees and
a pair of bridges arching uselessly over a dry riverbed. A
couple of Aborigines are lying on a patch of brown grass,
recumbent figures beside a smoking campfire. I have driven
to Anzac Hill. Almut did not want to come. The old
Telegraph Station is filled with photographs of pioneers and
camels. The overland line reached Alice Springs in 1872. All
they had to do after that was continue on to Darwin, and
from there to Java, so that they would eventually connect
to Europe. There are also photographs of an Aboriginal
gathering, a *corroboree*, which took place in 1905. 'Three hundred generations of Aranda, five generations of whites,'
someone has scrawled beneath it, and that is how it looks.
I peer at the mysterious paintings on the black bodies. The

men – there are four of them – stand with their hands behind their backs. The colours have lost their brilliance, and the old-fashioned photographic technique has reduced the landscape to a mere strip of blinking light, and there they are in all their glory, their bodies full of symbolic language, strings of white dots, snakes, labyrinthine shapes, riddles. They stand there in that long-gone moment, fraught with meaning, but I am unable to read the signs. I can see Alice Springs in the distance, looking small, insignificant, truly negligible, the way the earth must seem to our galaxy – a sigh, not even a comma. You can see the layout of the streets in the rudimentary grid and the place where the train tracks from the south came to a halt before going on to the tropical north, but beyond that bare minimum lies an endless landscape: plains, mountain peaks, the straight line of the lost road in the distance, the road we will take to Darwin. What do I remember of that road? The interminable dryness, the road trains – huge trucks consisting of three or more trailers that could toss a buffalo to the side of the road as if it were a dog – and a deer in a violent pool of blood. We left the Stuart Highway in a cloud of red dust. At first the ground was hard and rutted, making the car bounce all over the road, then it turned sandy and slippery. The rivers shown on the map were dry beds. And everywhere we went there were vicious gnats. I try to imagine barefooted people walking through that unbounded emptiness, but I cannot.

11

SOME PEOPLE ARE ACTUALLY TRANSPARENT. I SUPPOSE this is true of blacks too, but this one happened to be white, and as old as the hills. He wore a yellowed version of a pith helmet. From under it dripped — there is no other word for it — long strands of dirty white hair that merged with a broad, fan-shaped beard of the same colour. His skinny frame was clad in an outdated tropical uniform with ragged cuffs, out of which hung long, slender hands, with eerily long nails, more like claws. And yet the voice of the figure in the rocking chair was, in contrast to the rest, surprisingly high and melodious.

'You can close that book right now,' the voice said. 'Even if you spend the next ten years studying the subject, you won't understand it. I've lived here for fifty years, and I still don't get it. How much have you read – up to that bit about the moieties?'

He was right. I had been reading about the moieties on the way here and had not understood a thing. Or rather, I had understood the words, but not how it worked. I had already discovered that 'moiety' was derived from '*moitié*' and therefore meant half, but I still did not know what it had to do with the amazingly complex social life in the Aboriginal community: what someone from one half was not allowed to do with those in the other half, or who, on the other hand, was required to do what with those in the other group, or why someone in Arnhem Land belonged to the Dua moiety and his wife to the Yirritja moiety and what that meant in terms of rituals and ceremonies, or that these divisions were broken down into smaller units, dialect groups and clans, which in turn determined who was or who was not allowed to paint what and who could or could not sing which part of a song. Higher mathematics and Japanese court ceremonies were nothing compared to this. It made my head spin, so I gave up. Earlier that morning I had stopped to listen to those same songs being sung in a museum. Almut had walked rapidly on, but I had become entranced by the plaintive, repetitious songs sung by a group of older women, which seemed to go on forever. It was unlike anything I had ever heard before. A couple of old women with sun-scorched skins were standing on the sun-scorched red soil. Dust swirled up as they stomped their bare leathery feet and pounded their sticks on the hard dry ground, which seemed to be made of stone, while the melody went on and on, apparently repeating itself, and the words were so incomprehensible to me that you could hardly have believed it was a language, though that was the whole point: language, stories, ancestral beings who had crossed the sea in narrow boats and sung their way across the land on which I was standing, and had created the animals and spirits that would later become the totems that still governed the life of the people.

'Sit down over here.'

The voice commanded, and I obeyed. The face beneath the helmet seemed to be made of parchment, but the ice-blue eyes sparkled. He spoke the kind of English that marks a man of education and breeding. It was a miracle that he had managed to keep it up for fifty years. He was what the Australians refer to as a 'Pom'. His tropical uniform hung in such loose folds that he must have been almost a skeleton, but the voice gave the opposite impression. There was a signet ring on the little finger of his left hand. He too had his totem.

'My eyes are still good. I recognised the book you're reading. It was written a long time ago, and they say it's a masterpiece, but it won't help you. I recognised it the moment I saw those abstract drawings, those numbered and lettered lines that are supposed to explain the secret world of the indigenous peoples. Most admirable, and also accurate. It will tell you who is allowed to marry whom, who is allowed to take part in the ceremony in which a body is smoked before a burial, who is not allowed to sing when the bones are reburied, who is descended from the maternal line and who from the paternal line, going back

God knows how many generations . . . and at the end you'll know everything there is to know and promptly forget it. You're not an anthropologist, are you?'

'No.'

'I thought not. Even if you read that book from cover to cover, you would still look at their society and know nothing. I'm not trying to make it sound even more mysterious than it already is, but it *is* mysterious, as well as being beautiful. Well, perhaps that doesn't apply to the people. Praxiteles would not have taken any one of them for a model . . . or us, for that matter. Apparently they do not correspond to our ideal of beauty, though I stopped looking at it that way long ago. I find them beautiful. The antiquity of their world is what makes them beautiful. For me at least. Along with the things they produce: their songs, their art. They live their art – there is no difference between the way they live, the way they think and the things they make. It's a bit like our own Middle Ages, before everything fell apart. It's easier to live in a closed world. That's what attracts you people, if you don't mind my saying so. "You people" doesn't sound very polite, but I have lived for years out here in the back of beyond, where I have watched you people come in search of answers. It's everything all rolled into one, poetry, a total way of life. For people coming from a place of chaos and confusion, it's quite tempting. Especially since it has been destroyed, or almost. That is what everyone has always been looking for, isn't it? A lost paradise?

'They dreamed an endless dream, an eternity in which they continued to live forever and in which nothing would have had to change. Once upon a time creatures who had dreamed the world had come and now they themselves were allowed to go on dreaming in a world ruled by spirits and filled with enchanted places – a magical system in which we do not have a place, even if we wanted to be a part of it.'

I said nothing. From the hall on the other side of the porch came the erratic stutter of old-fashioned ceiling fans. I already knew what he was telling me, but I wanted to go on listening to that voice for as long as I could. He spoke in a strange sing-song, a kind of lament, though oddly enough it did not make you feel sad. And maybe he was telling me something I wanted to hear – that I could do without all of this, without the erudition and the explanations, that I could simply let it all wash over me without my understanding it, the way we used to do back in our room in Jardins, when we let ourselves be seduced by the images. Surely the dancing women in the museum had nothing to do with those diagrams, graphs and abstractions; at any rate they would not help me solve the puzzle, and perhaps I should not expect them to. What I had to remember were the rock paintings, the landscapes, the hoarse whisper of a person who, during our first night together, had lifted me out of my life by uttering words I had not understood, just as I had not understood the words of the songs I had listened to this morning, though I would take them with me for all time.

I put the book aside.

'Good. I wasn't talking through my hat just now. I know, because I'm the one who wrote the book.'

I stared at him. The picture on the back was of a young man, flanked by two hunters with spears. Cyril Clarence. He looked like a young James Mason. The picture must have been taken at least sixty years ago. When I told him that, he laughed.

'I have no regrets, but I've devoted half a century of my life to trying to grasp what it is that makes their world tick.'

'And have you found out?'

He didn't answer. Instead, he picked up the book, which I had laid on the table beside him, unfolded the map in the back, and pointed to a place about a hundred miles east of Darwin. I didn't see any roads leading to it.

When I said that, he laughed again. 'There are now. Well, dirt tracks. You've got to have a 4x4, and even then it has to be the right season. In the old days people used to walk there. I had a friend who lived there.'

'Not any more?'

'No, not any more. He was murdered. He was a painter, and a hunter. He built an airstrip there, more or less with his bare hands. He was part of a small community. They had gone back to their ancestral land. Sacred sites, secret spots, forbidden places: you are allowed to forget a lot of things, but those you have to remember. Because even though you cannot see it, there is an enchanted world there with enchanted plants and enchanted animals, a landscape full of invisible clues. That is all you need to know. He was killed by his son-in-law. I used to visit him from time to time. He told me quite a few things. I also used to talk to him on a ham radio. I thought they were living in paradise, but I was wrong. It wasn't there either. He made beautiful things. Every once in a while one of those gallery people would fly over and pick something up. He earned a lot of money that way. The fact that his work was exhibited in museums in America was of little interest to him. Nor did he ever feel like explaining the iconography in any detail. He was wise enough to realise that the strangers who saw his work either could not understand its magical significance or did not want to, and that they only bought his work as decorative objects or as investments. For the rest he lived off his hunting. He was a fantastic hunter and fisherman.'

'Why was he killed?'

'Out of jealousy. It's still the real world, even here. You have to be very strong to cope with so many changes. He was strong, but things frequently go wrong. Our world is ruled by greed.'

'What happened to the man who killed him?'

'Hand me the map, would you? Here, do you see that? Endless brown plains. And no roads anywhere. Hundreds and hundreds of miles of empty space. There is only one dirt track that goes to the Nganyalala outpost, a hundred or so miles to the east. It's surrounded by a vast emptiness, nothing but bush and flood plains. They can hole up there for years, if they have to. He took his elderly mother with him. She knew how to survive in the wilderness. Where you and I see nothing but desert, she will see water. So long as you know how to read the world. Roots and berries, small animals. In any case neither of them was ever found. Where are you making for?'

'To the Sickness Dreaming Place.'

'For any particular reason?'

'Yes.'

'Hmm. It won't be easy.' He pointed to the map. 'Here. The Sleisbeck mine.' Written beside it was the word 'abandoned'. 'You're not officially allowed into this area. It has always been a problem. When Leichhardt entered the South Alligator Valley in 1845, he had a lot of trouble with the Jawoyn who were living there. They think of it as sacred ground. The ancestor spirit who rules over it does not want the earth to be disturbed, otherwise something terrible is bound to happen. Of course the reason it's called Sickness Country is because of the natural radioactivity found there. Sacred ground is one thing, uranium mines are another. Since 1950 mining companies have been extracting gold, uranium, palladium, and God knows what else. Australia's national debt versus poisoned mine water, vanishing animal species, sacred land rights, ancestral myths – it's already an explosive enough mix. Not to mention all those beautiful rock paintings. Lascaux is nothing in comparison.'

Just then Almut came sailing in from the patio, waving a newspaper. She flopped down in a chair without acknowledging Cyril. Nothing ever surprised Almut, not even the fact that you were talking to a centenarian.

'Here, take a look at this! It makes you realise you're somewhere else! "Clan Elders Sing Aborigine to Death". I've been trying to imagine how they did it. I know that sounds can be used to torture people. I've been told that the steady dripping of water in a bucket can drive a person insane. But singing? If it's anything like what we heard this morning in the museum – that slow drone – it might just do the trick. After all, it drove me nuts too. How you could go on listening to it is beyond me. I could feel the vibrations of those low tones down around my knees. A kind of buzzing.' She imitated the sound of a drill.

'What's your friend saying?' Cyril asked. 'I love your language, it's beautiful, but I don't understand a word.'

I told him, and he began to laugh.

Suddenly Almut seemed to see him for the first time. She shot me an enquiring glance and said, 'Where'd you dig *him* up? I didn't know people like that still existed! He looks like something straight out of a movie. Why did he laugh?'

'Sing a person to death,' Cyril said. 'It would be nice if one could actually do that. It has an entirely different meaning here, however, though in the end I suppose it boils down to the same thing. It's what happens when someone is placed outside the community, for whatever reason – for stealing a totem from someone else or breaking another important taboo. He or she is then cast out. The ban itself is sung. Once you've been banished, no one in the group is allowed to help you in any way. You might as well be dead. Those are the people you see hanging around the big cities. They're no longer part of a community.'

Almut said nothing. She seemed to be disappointed by the story. She stood up. 'Another illusion down the drain,' she said. 'What were you two talking about before I got here?'

'Sleisbeck. Cyril says it isn't straightforward.'

She immediately picked up on his name, as if she had heard it a hundred times before.

'Then Cyril ought to tell us how to get there.'

'He says it's impossible. We should go somewhere else. Ubirr. Kakadu. Nourlangie.'

The three of us pore over the map. His hand, as he points out the places, looks as if it is made of transparent marble.

'But what do we do about your Sickness Dreaming Place?'

'I've been cured already.'

12

AS WE ARE DRIVING OFF THE NEXT DAY, WE SEE HIM standing on the patio. Our Japanese clunker makes a God-awful noise, but we are in high spirits. Almut sings half the repertoire of Maria Bethania. From time to time a road train sweeps us to the side while the drivers laugh and shout and make obscene gestures. It is October, so the rainy season, known here as 'the Wet', has begun, though the big rainstorms are not due until later. After twenty-five miles, we turn left in the direction of Arnhem Land. Almut chants the names: Humpty Doo, Annaburro, Wildman Lagoon. Somewhere we are supposed to choose between Jabiru and Ja Ja, but I can't find the turning on the map, and then the road fizzles out into a red track and the track becomes an endless repetition of itself, with the dread and silent forest all around us.

We get out of the vehicle beside a river. The silence is broken by unknown sounds. 'CROCODILES FREQUENT THIS AREA. KEEP CHILDREN AND DOGS AWAY FROM THE WATER'S EDGE.' I stare at the gleaming black surface, at the red soil beneath my feet, at the dry eucalyptus leaves, curled into the shapes of letters as if they had been shaken from a tray of type. There is very little traffic on this road, so we are alone in our cloud of dust. The few cars coming towards us can be seen from miles off, like clouds or apparitions. I feel happy. When we finally get to Ubirr, it takes us about an hour to walk to the site.

'Majesty,' Almut murmurs. I look at her to see what she means. She points at the view and puts an arm around me, as though she wants to protect me. But from what?

'It's all so old,' she says at last. 'It makes me feel ancient too, as if I've been here forever. Time is nothing. A mere fart. Someone could blow us away with a single puff. What's a thousand years? Nothing at all. If we were to come back, we wouldn't know ourselves. We'd have the same brains, but different software. I know what I'm talking about, because I've been staring much too long into the eyes of the Abos. Doesn't it bother you? For a thousand years, or even ten thousand years, the same eyes, the same landscape. They are their own eternity, but no one can endure that for very long.' Then she laughs and says, 'Fired for being too solemn.' But she is right. Everything – the stones, the trees, the rocks – do their best to thrust their antiquity at you, there is not a single human voice to distract you, and intruders are scared off by the malevolent gleam of the stones – no wonder they think this ground is sacred. The murmur of bushes, the rustle of invisible creatures. This is where they lived, seeking shelter beneath this overhang. Down the sides of the cliff and high above their heads they painted the animals they lived off. Later I write down the names: *barramundi*, the big fish; *badjalanga*, the long-necked turtle; *kalekale*, the catfish; *budjudu*, the iguana.

'I've got to lie down,' Almut says. 'I'm getting a crick in my neck.'

I lie beside her.

'Too bad you can't do this in the Sistine Chapel,' she says, but I have already drifted off. I feel as if I am lying in a giant Mycenaean vase: imagined fish swimming downstream, the draughtsmanship of such delicacy, the tiny white figures beside it so humble, so faceless, as if to say they were not really there. The longer I look, the more I see that the cliff is composed of hundreds of colours. Weather, erosion, mould, time – everything has taken root in this stony surface, on top of which has been drawn an image of something that was real, a living reality, which had to be filtered through a person in order to be recreated in the colours of the earth, immovable, recorded, etched in time.

I would like to say something, but I am not sure I can put it into words, something about what Almut just said, about time being a mere fart, but she is the only one who can say things like that. Whatever I blurt out sounds confused and stilted. 'According to Cyril,' I say, 'these rock paintings are twenty thousand years old – a number that is no longer just a series of zeros, but something as tangible as the fabric, the weave, of the clothes on my back, so that what I see and what I am are in the same continuum, which does away with time like a conjuror's cloth, abolishing it, declaring it null and void, turning it into an element like water or air, something that leaves you free to enter it wherever you are, not just in the direction where your part of it ends.'

'Whoa! Slow down,' Almut says, but by this time we have got up and walked to the lookout above the cliff. Below us the landscape stretches to the end of the visible world. It is a dream landscape, which ought to be filled with the figures of gods. A bird of prey hangs above it, motionless, as if it were its sole guardian. Other birds, white, are floating in a marshy pool near the edge of the woods. Beneath us, at the foot of the rocks, I see the pointed pyramids of termite mounds, sand palms as unspectacular as grass, rocks as the building blocks of a destroyed temple.

'I wasn't making fun of you,' Almut says. 'I know what you mean, I just wouldn't put it in quite those words. It has something to do with melancholy, but also with triumph.'

'Yes,' I say, and I would like to add that the triumph comes from realising – if only for a moment – that you are at once mortal and immortal, but I don't say it. 'Time is a fart' is a lot snappier, and maybe it boils down to the same thing. 'The landscape you are going to see is sixty million years old,' Cyril had said. Yellow Water, Alligator River, ashen colours, mottled white gum trees in moss-green wetlands, traces of a dead river, a bleeding cliff, where a monster has bitten a chunk out of the earth. We have seen enough, it is time to leave. Once, long ago, we began this journey in a room in São Paulo. Now, at last, we have arrived.

13

HOW MUCH THINKING CAN YOU DO WITHOUT EVER leaving the room? I took a trip in my head and ended up back where I started – in the stillness. The person who met the man in the gallery, now lying at my side, was no longer the same person who had arrived six months ago in Sydney. I suppose I should say, '*I* was no longer the same,' and I wish I could, but a gap has been created between me and myself, and I haven't yet learned how to bridge the distance. Almut says, 'You're in love, simple as that,' but I'm not. It is much more than that. It is getting something as well as giving something up. I am not going to stay with this man, because he will not be staying with me. He made that clear from the start, and that has to do with distance too. He is just as inaccessible as his paintings. You can hang them on the wall, all right, but they are not yours, and they never will be, because they come from a place to which you have no access. The problem is not that I do not fit into his world, or that he would never take me to wherever he comes from, or that he is ashamed of me, or for whatever reason will not present me to the people he is closest to, nor is it the fact that he took me, like an ordinary tourist, to a place where Aboriginal life was presented as a kind of theatre, complete with bush tucker and didgeridoo, campfires and clumsy dancing that bore no resemblance to the dancing I had seen in the museum in Darwin, which meant that he had either underestimated me or insulted me, though there was no point in talking about it since he doesn't talk. I don't care. Perhaps he was trying to make something clear to me, something I would rather not know. But when night falls and the nonsense is done with, we are alone again with the silence and immensely few words. I never knew words could be so few and far between. But that is fine with me. Or is it? Is there such a thing as pornography without the porn? Simply an idea in your head, without a graphic image? Pure pornography of the mind, or of a situation, in which a lie changes every move, kiss, caress and climax into something else, something obscene and perverse? I think about this, and yet at the same time I lie here and wait for him to utter one of his infrequent words, for him to touch me again and make me forget my thoughts.

Almut made some kind of remark about my 'noble savage', and for the first time in years I was furious with her. Not at the insult, but at her lack of understanding. She has always understood how I feel, but now I had all of a sudden lost her. It has nothing to do with being in love. It is much worse than that. More obscene, more perverse. If I am in love with anything, it is with a cliff or an expanse of desert.

It all started with his painting. I stood there in front of it, not knowing what to make of it. It was unlike anything else I had seen on our trip. There were no figures, no sign of any creatures which, no matter how strange, were in some way recognisable. Instead, there was a defiant, impenetrable black with a shimmer of light glinting through it − a contradiction that drew me into the blackness, exactly as I was later drawn to the artist. But none of these words bring me any closer to the matter at hand. To an outsider, it must have seemed ordinary enough. At a private viewing, you stare at a painting too long, tune out everything around you, the voices, the people, think the forbidden phrase 'like a black cloud', wish you could block it all out, the violence, the horror, the fear, and feel yourself being sucked back into that cloud, as though you had never travelled to and across a country that had been the stuff of your childhood dreams, but instead had travelled straight to this painting as if to an exorcism, an exorcism that can occur only if I let myself be sucked back into the taboo. Tears flow down my cheeks, but luckily no one can see them since I am standing with my back to the crowd. What they do see if they are looking this way is the gallery owner coming over to me, saying, 'You seem to be quite interested in that painting,' catching sight of my tears and beating a hasty retreat after a mumbled, 'I'll introduce you to the painter,' and only coming back with him much later, after I have dried my tears, which well up again when he is standing before me because he himself *is* his painting. All that has to do with the pain of healing – so much I understand. I say nothing, not even to Almut. I expect nothing, I have surrendered myself to it. The gallery owner must have told him something, because he stood there before me without saying a word, whether out of shyness or because his thoughts were miles away I couldn't tell. And I still can't. Sometimes I think he doesn't see me, that even when he touches me or has sex with me, I am invisible to him, someone without a soul, a mere shape or figure – and he is right about that – as if what we do has no substance, as if his pre-announced departure can be felt in everything, in his long silences, his stillness, his refusal to see me although I am dying to be seen and know I won't be – I knew all that the moment I saw the painting.

That is all there is to tell. The week he granted me is almost over. The gallery owner, who was drunk by the end of the evening, said to me, 'I'm only lending him to you. Take good care of him. And for God's sake don't ask him about his paintings. He's not allowed to talk about them. It's too complicated to explain. Taboos, secrets, totems – a whole world you'd be better off not knowing about.' He gave us the key to his cabin by the ocean in Port Willunga. On the first day, we walked along the shore, an endless walk. It was high tide, and I had the feeling that the surf was roaring just for me, as if to make up for the silent figure at my side. From time to time he pointed out a bird and told me what it was called. Otherwise, he didn't say a word. Only a brief statement at the beginning, uttered without looking at me, as a kind of Declaration of Independence, that at the end of the week he would be 'going back to my mob', without even mentioning which part of Australia they lived in. We walked until dark, then went back to the cabin. He was familiar with it, had obviously been there before. And obviously with other women. He did not switch on the light, but put his hand, the fingers spread wide, on the nape of my neck. Even though it was the lightest of touches, I could feel how calloused his fingers were. Surely it isn't possible for someone to touch you so lightly and yet give you a feeling of being lifted? The next thing I knew I was being rocked — there is no other word for it — a kind of endless rocking that blended in with the sound of the surf, the heave and swell of the ocean, which wrapped me in its embrace until I felt myself flow away and no longer needed to exist. When I woke up the next morning, he was gone. I looked out of the window and saw him sitting in the early rays of the sun, a dark silhouette in the sand, motionless as a rock, and knew at once that I had substituted one memory for another and that this one would leave me with as little peace as the other one had. I would exist in someone else's mind, without knowing who I was in there. This would have been unbearable to me in the past, but it didn't matter to me any more. I now knew who *I* was. One time, acting on a bizarre impulse, I had asked my mother what she would like to be thinking of at the moment of her death.

She didn't answer right away, but merely shook her head. Then at last she said, 'Some things are better left unsaid.'

'Can't you tell even your own daughter?' I asked.

'Especially not my own daughter,' she said.

After a few days in Port Willunga we went to a strange place, a reserve in which we played at being Aborigines. It sounds awful, and it was. I don't know why he took me there, but at least I now know how to find food in the desert and have seen how pure silence can turn you into silence yourself. No one was surprised to see me, so perhaps he had brought others there before. I shrugged off the well-meaning nonsense and practised withdrawing into myself – I'm good at that. It was not his mob, and since they spoke English to him, they did not come from the same language group either. I did see him smile, but not at me. I considered telling him what had happened to me that week, but my black cloud could never be his. I would take it with me when I left, incorporate it into the rest of my life, as if one cloud could cancel out another. We'll see. It is our last night together. I rub my hand over the dirt floor of the cabin. It feels hard and dry, like paper. Everything in this country is different from mine. Outside, the dawn's early light flows out over the world with such violence that it almost hurts my eyes. Red paint. Blood. I roll over and look at him. He is still asleep. He too just a shape. I wish I could lift him up and fly away with him, over the vast emptiness of this country, to the place he comes from, to the place where he belongs and I do not.

14

'DIDN'T YOU AT LEAST HAVE A FEW LAUGHS TOGETHER?'
Almut asked. I knew she was going to ask me that. I also
knew that she was angry, indignant. If there is no laughter,
something is wrong. In Almut's book, at any rate. I had
come back to Adelaide alone. We still had one night left in
the cabin in Port Willunga, and she wanted to see it. The
same beach, the same ocean, the same birds, though now
I knew what they were called. We were sitting high up on
a dune in a little restaurant called the Star of Greece because
a ship by that name had once been shipwrecked there. It
was high tide again, and the surf still had many things to
say. Unlike me. I knew that Almut was waiting for me to tell
her everything, since our relationship had always been based
on sharing. We had no secrets from each other. But I also
knew that I could not talk to her. Not yet.

'What did you do this week?' I asked her at last.

'Me? I partied every night, OK? No . . . I spent all my time
wondering what I ought to do next. I didn't know if you
were coming back.'

'I said I'd be back at the end of the week, didn't I?'

'Yes, but the expression on your face might have meant the exact opposite: that you would never want to come back.'

I shrugged, but she blew up. I knew that my best bet was to wait out the storm.

'Why can't you admit that we've got a problem? For one thing, we've run out of money, though that's beside the point. I didn't know how you were doing, and I'm not used to that. I was worried. Not because the man took no notice of me, but because I don't think he saw you either.

'His work is beautiful, especially the painting you were so crazy about. I've forgotten the title, but if you labelled it "The Gates of Hell" you wouldn't be far wrong. No wonder the guy never laughs. Actually, I never see any of them laugh.'

'Them?'

'You're right, I'm sorry. But one night in Alice Springs, when you were asleep, I wandered off and got lost. I didn't tell you.'

'What happened?'

'Nothing. But I found myself face to face with three of these great big guys. They stopped, I stopped. They reeked of beer. That's all. They stood there staring at me until finally I turned and walked away. End of story.'

She paused, then added, 'It was all so sad.'

'You can see the same sadness in São Paulo.'

'No, not the same. For one thing, there's always laughter

in São Paulo, no matter how terrible things are. Our slaves came from Africa, so at least they know how to dance. Really dance, I mean. Can you imagine a samba school here? But that's not what I meant. It's all so hopeless. Do you know that Groucho Marx joke? "We were standing on the edge of a precipice. Since then, we have taken a giant leap forward." Even that was denied them. They were snatched away long before they got to the edge. Anyway, half of it is fake.'

'What's fake?'

'Everything. They used to paint their bodies or draw pictures in the sand. It meant something, and then it was gone. A bit of wind, and the drawing was swept away. Nothing was for sale. If I buy a piece of painted bark that was once given to the dead, how can I be sure it's worth anything? How many of them can one person make? And then what happens? Do they sit out there in the bush with their secret whatevers, waiting for another gallery owner with bags of money to land his Piper Cub on their airstrip?'

'You're disappointed.'

'Maybe. And maybe I'm right.'

'Because our precious dream has been shattered? And yet a week ago in Ubirr you were in ecstasy. Or have you forgotten already?'

'No, I haven't forgotten. But I can't help feeling that somehow or other it's all doomed. And then when you disappeared like that . . .'

'I didn't disappear.'

'No, but you looked terribly unhappy ...'

'I wasn't unhappy. I was just ... somewhere else. Trying to work something out.'

She laid a hand on my arm. 'OK, I'll stop asking questions. I'm sorry. But the least you can do is make me laugh. Tell me a funny word, and then I'll tell you my news. We've had an offer that ought to make you laugh. At any rate I hope so. But first a funny word.'

'*Maku.*'

'*Maku*,' she repeated. When am I supposed to start laughing?'

'As soon as you know what it means.'

'Use it in a sentence.'

'"Out in the desert I ate delicious *maku*." Witchetty grubs — the larvae of ghost moths — and beetles. They can be found near mulga trees, along with *tjala*, honey ants. You can dig them up underneath a mulga tree after it has rained. The ants swell up to the size of frogs. They're full of a yellowy, sickeningly sweet nectar that's meant for the worker ants. They come over and suck it up. You see, I've learned a lot. Send me into the desert, and I'll survive. So what's this about an offer?'

'It's in Perth. That's miles away, but I think our junk heap can just about make it. There's going to be a literary festival with a couple of theatre performances. They're looking for angels, or rather extras dressed up as angels.'

'To act in a play?'

'No. I'm not sure I really understand it, but the way they explained it to me was that while the festival is going on, angels will be hidden all over the city. People are supposed to go and look for them.'

'What do we have to do?'

'Nothing. They give us a pair of wings and every day for a week someone picks us up and takes us to a hiding place in a church, or in a ruin, or in a bank. We just have to stay put all day and let people find us. Somehow it's all related to *Paradise Lost*.'

'Never read it. No, wait, we had to read it at school, but I've forgotten most of it. There's an angel with a flaming sword who expels Adam and Eve from Paradise.'

'God, that's right. Plus Satan. The first book, about Satan's hatred of God, goes on forever. And then there's Eve, who thinks she's supposed to eat the apple. All very sad, but I don't remember exactly what happens, not in any detail.'

'Me neither. So what do we do when people find us?'

'They're not allowed to talk to us. They will, of course, but we're not supposed to answer. And we have to stay perfectly still. Anyway, the pay's good.'

'How did you hear about it?'

'There was an ad in the theatre section of the paper here. I gave them a call. They're going to hold auditions. I'm sure they'll take you, but it'll be a bit harder for me.' She pointed to her breasts. 'Have you ever seen an angel with boobs?'

15

SO NOW I'M AN ANGEL. IT WASN'T DIFFICULT. THE
director picked me out of the line-up straight away. 'The
thing is,' she said, 'you have to be able to lie very still.'
Turning to her assistant, she added, 'She's so small she
could fit inside the cupboard in that building on William
Street, by the Gledden Arcade. Make a note of that.'

And then to me, 'Do you think you can lie very still?
Because that's what you'll have to do.'

I said it would not be a problem. After all, I had enough
to think about. Almut also passed with flying colours. She
had done her best to hide her breasts, but she need not
have bothered. 'We'll put her on the roof of His Majesty's
Theatre, across from Wilson's Car Park. She looks like she
could hold a sword in the air for a couple of hours.'

Yesterday was our first day. Last night Almut was so tired
she couldn't think straight.

'I have to stand all day in that bloody sun, but the view's
fantastic. Mind you, I don't see any of the people up close.
How about you?'

'I don't see them either.'

I don't see them, but I can hear them. I listen to the way they walk up the stairs, then stop and stand still for a moment until they see me. I can always tell when they have spotted me, I can feel it, which is strange because there is never more than one of them at a time. They have to promise to look for the angels alone. I try to guess from the footsteps whether it's a man or a woman, since I am not allowed to turn round. I have to curl up on the floor of the cupboard with my face to the wall. Whenever someone comes in, I try to hold my breath for as long as I can, but after a while you get incredibly stiff and the wings are fastened so tightly that it starts to hurt like mad. Thank God I can always hear them coming up the stairs, so when there is a lull I rotate my shoulders. Otherwise I would go crazy. The other thing that annoys me are the people who deliberately stand there for a long time, hoping you will break down and turn round. It's always a man, you can tell. When that happens, I concentrate on my favourite Annunciations – on the poses, the position of the wings. And I think of *him*, of how we lay there together in the desert, also on the ground. Too bad I didn't have my wings then. I wish I knew whether he has been thinking of me, and where he is. And then I fantasise a bit about what he would say if he walked in here, and whether I would recognise his step and turn round, even though it's against the rules, but of course that is ridiculous. I discovered afterwards where his mob lives. It wasn't hard to work out because they have a very distinctive style. The whole kinship group paints in the same way. Here in the museum in Perth, I have seen the paintings of the rest of his mob, the people I was hoping to meet, though they were kept secret from me, or perhaps it is the other way round, since of course my existence was kept secret from them. Time passes quickly when you've got so much to think about. The wall of my cupboard holds no secrets from me – I know every last crack, scratch and paint mark. My mind wanders through it like a walker in an empty landscape. When no one is there, I sing softly to myself. After a while you go into a kind of trance, or dream that you can fly. It gets really crazy at the end of the day when the bus comes to pick us up. It is full of angels – a really motley bunch. We each have our own way of coping: coke, tranquillisers, maths problems. We are all exhausted and bubbling over with stories. The angels in full view have a particularly hard time, because people say the strangest things to them: declarations of love, abuse, obscenities. They know we are not allowed to react, and some people seem to get really turned on by that.

Almut and I have said nothing more about the week I was away. I keep those days locked inside me. Sometimes I think about what we will do next, and whether we should stay in this country. I know that Almut would like to go home, but I am not ready to leave. What I would really like to do is to go into the desert on my own, but I do not dare say that to Almut. In the evenings, when she is downstairs in the hotel bar, I unwrap the painting, put it on the table and lean it against the wall. Then I sit across from it, like a nun at her devotions. After a few minutes, it starts to have an effect, and I feel a longing that I can't put into words, but that I know will be part of me forever. I don't want to say anything to Almut, at least not yet, and though I am not sure this is something you can decide, I think I will always be a wanderer, so I can make the world my desert. I have enough food for thought to last a lifetime. There are honey ants and grubs wherever you go, or else roots and berries, and now I know how to find them. I can survive.

PART TWO

PART TWO

1

ALL WE NEED IS A CITY ON THE WATER, THE MONTH OF January, a day of sleet, a station. Grey is the best of all colours: a hidden sun saving its warmth for the other side of the world and the stories written there. Thirteen train platforms, some more crowded than others. And then the divining rod – that indispensable tool of our trade – begins to home in on a specific direction, twitching and jerking until it clearly points to a loosely assembled group of travellers: the walk-ons, the extras. We are not sure whether they have been assigned roles today. After all, we are not the only ones in this line of work, and they might be characters in someone else's story. The chap in the brown jacket? No. The young mother with the toddler? No. Not those three soldiers either. The man in the funny-looking hat is too old – he would only complicate matters. But we had better hurry, the train should have been here by now. Ah, that chap over there, the one standing behind the man – obviously from Bavaria – who is reading the *Bildzeitung*, he is the one we need, he is clearly our man. Wind-blown wisps of thinning hair, eyes watering from the cold. No, not the one behind him, he's no use to us, you're looking at the wrong person, I mean the other one, the man who has looked at his watch twice already. He will do. Suede shoes – an English make, a bit worn, though – cotton trousers in a drab army colour, a grey loden coat and a red scarf, which is cashmere at least. There is an inherent contrast in all those textiles, in terms of both colour and age: a touch of the artist, an off-duty army captain, a man who goes to watch his daughter play hockey in a ritzy town like Laren, with the various items of clothing cancelling each other out, as if the wearer was not sure who he really wanted to be and was using the defiant red of the scarf to try and mask his uncertainty. OK, let's take a closer look. Some women might find this man attractive, though he probably is not at his best today. He looks around, to see if someone is coming, but he can forget it. The train has just passed Haarlem, so let us get started. Mixing people's lives together, if only for a short while, is no small matter. Some elements, just as in chemistry, attract each other, and others repel. Lives actually need long preparation. Just like food. Hmm, you are right, there does not seem to be a chef, unless you want to think of life itself as one big culinary experiment, and why not? In any case, the chemistry is far from easy. One life takes longer to cook than another, the stoves are located in different parts of the world, the result is uncertain. Our metaphor is wearing thin, so we have only this to say: life — to use this ridiculous analogy one last time — is the stupidest of culinary experiments. For the most part this leads to human suffering, but every once in a while — though not very often — literature profits by it. We shall see.

2

ERIK ZONDAG WAS NOT SURE EXACTLY WHAT MOOD HE
was in when he boarded the train to Austria, which was
hardly surprising. It was cold, he was feeling under the
weather, and he did not know what to expect, other than
that he was on his way to a health spa that his friend Arnold
Pessers had recommended. Arnold, like Erik, had reached
that unmapped area described by poets as a 'dark wood'
and by doctors as 'midlife' – an absurd label, especially since
the end date is generally unknown. If the end occurs earlier than the statistical norm, 'midlife' ought to shift along
with it, so that in some cases it was already far behind you
and you did not even know it, a reflection that did not
make Erik Zondag any more cheerful. The train was late.
Through the dirty glass roof of Amsterdam's Central
Station, he could see the gusty winds blowing sleet across
the water of the IJ. It was Friday, and still too early to buy
the newspaper for which he worked as a literary critic, which
meant that he could not read the printed review in which
he had savaged the latest novel of one of Holland's literary

giants. Some writers did not age gracefully; after a while you knew all of their mannerisms and obsessions. There was not enough dying going on in Dutch literature. Reve, Mulisch, Claus, Nooteboom and Wolkers had all been writing when he was in his cradle, and it did not look as if they were ever going to stop. He could only conclude that they took the idea of immortality much too literally. His girlfriend Anja – an art editor at a rival paper – had accused him of writing an unfair review.

'You're in a bad mood because you're going off on your journey tomorrow.'

'That has nothing to do with it. I've known the man my whole life. By now I feel as if I could write his books myself.'

'So why don't you? Maybe you'll even earn some decent money for a change.'

Anja was eighteen years his junior, and that was inexcusable. They had been living together for the last four years – if you could call it that, because they both still lived in their own apartments: hers in Amsterdam Noord and his in Oud Zuid, which tended to complicate their daily lives somewhat. She thought that his place looked and felt like the basket of 'an ageing dog', while he thought that her eighth-floor high-rise overlooking the polder had all the charm of a laboratory. Bare, white and spotless, not really where you would want to spend the night for fun. After all, he thought, it was better to do what had brought you together in the first place in a dog basket rather than in a laboratory. But Anja disagreed. In fact, it occurred to him now, she had been disagreeing with him more and more lately. Yesterday's conversation about the review had also ended disastrously.

'If you ask me, you're jealous of the man.'

'Jealous? Of that conceited fathead?'

'He's conceited, all right. But at least he can write.'

'Your paper gave him a bad review too.'

'That may be, but at least it was subtle. Yours was unmixed venom.'

There was no question of making love after that. Dutch authors had a lot to answer for.

'It's high time you went to that spa.' This was her conclusion the next morning. 'You've been moping around for ages!' That was true. An unshaven man going on fifty who finds himself staring out over the endless melancholy of the polder at seven thirty on a January morning is aware of this, especially when the radio announces that twelve more Palestinians have been shot in the Gaza Strip, that the stock market has surely bottomed out by now, and that the latest attempt to form a new cabinet has reached a deadlock.

'I'm not in the mood for a spa. It's a ridiculous amount of money to pay for a week of fasting.'

'You won't get anywhere with an attitude like that. This is your chance to shed those excess kilos you're always going on about. Besides, Arnold says he came back a different man.'

'Is that what you want?'

'What?'

'A different man. Am I supposed to become a new person at my age? I'm just beginning to get used to myself.'

'You might be, but I'm not. You depress the hell out of me sometimes. Besides that, you drink too much!'

He did not bother to reply. At the crossroads below, a white delivery van had manoeuvred itself with geometrical precision into the side of a pale blue Honda.

'Arnold is looking a whole lot better. And he hasn't had a drop to drink since he got back.'

'That's because he's too busy moaning about all the food he's not allowed to eat.'

No, that conversation had not gone well either. He looked at his watch. Just then, the loudspeaker announced that his train would be delayed for another few minutes. In point of fact, he was not sure why he had chosen to take this train. To catch the night train to Innsbruck, he had to change trains in Duisburg, and something about the name 'Duisburg' had appealed to him. It conjured up something cold and grey, a German city still smelling faintly of a long-ago war – an atmosphere of hardship and suffering that matched his present mood.

3

HE WAS RIGHT. DUISBURG WAS AS COLD AS AMSTERDAM. The threat of war that he had earlier glimpsed in a fellow passenger's *Bildzeitung* was broadcast here from every news-stand in huge red and black letters. He walked aimlessly around the city and realised that this had unconsciously been his intention. Why did it always take him so long to work things out? He had phoned Anja, but she had not answered and he had not left a message. The German train had left on time. He had installed himself in his single berth and been awakened from time to time by the broadcast of metallic voices on deserted platforms and the plaintive cries of the train, which had not been at all unpleasant. He liked travelling by train. His berth swayed gently, the invisible drummer on the rails beneath him beat a fabulous rhythm, and before falling asleep he had felt reasonably happy for the first time that day. Why he had let himself be talked into this ridiculous adventure, God only knew, but Arnold Pessers had been rather convincing. He had gone on for hours about how light he had felt on his return from the spa. Now that he thought about it, ever since his return Arnold had become pretty much of a bore. The two of them were about the same age and knew each other's stories. Once, when Arnold was in Japan, he had fallen madly in love with a model he met in connection with his work as a photographer. The whole thing had ended badly, as was to be expected. Stormy romances might flourish in TV dramas, but they were only tiresome in real life. Arnold's friends had had their work cut out for them, but after two years of serious alcohol abuse, the photographer had eventually pulled himself together. Why people went on making the same mistakes over and over was a mystery. Erik shuddered. Imagine never being able to have another drink. That must be about the worst thing that could happen to you. A day never went by in which he did not have at least a couple of drinks. In strictly medical terms, that made you an alcoholic, but he never got drunk nor actually had a hangover, and whenever he went in for a check-up, his lab tests were fine. 'I know,' Arnold had said, 'but it'll catch up with you sooner or later.' And Arnold had started rhapsodising again about his new life, his regenerated liver, his lost flab, his new-found energy and his amazing diet, which was based on several monastic rules – totally incomprehensible to Erik – in which certain foods were not allowed to be eaten in combination with certain others, lettuce was taboo at night, eating fruit after dinner was a deadly sin ('because it'll rot in your stomach'), smoking was out of the question, hard liquor was a form of suicide and wine a medicine rather than a harmless pleasure. One or two glasses were the absolute limit. My God, he was going to die of boredom. But one thing was indisputable: Arnold had lost a lot of weight.

He woke up around seven. It was now or never – the train was due to get in an hour from now. They were speeding past mountains, pockets of mist, villages, houses in which the lights were already on and people were moving in and out of the rooms. In Innsbruck he put his bags in a locker. Arnold had told him how to catch the Blue Train to Igls, but he was in no hurry. He wanted to walk around a bit first. And maybe look for Café Zentral, which Arnold had recommended as a nice old-fashioned Austrian café, the type of place in which Thomas Bernhard would have sat and read his newspaper. Erik liked Thomas Bernhard, not only because, like the Dutch author W. F. Hermans, he had perfected the art of ranting and raving, but because, also like Hermans, his anger seemed to stem from an embittered, disappointed love. He particularly admired the style of the tirade – the urgent, passionate, rhetorical anger with its secret, and often invisible, ingredient: the compassion with which the Austrian wrote about his surroundings, about his country and his own life, which he himself had referred to as 'a life dedicated to death'.

In the café he read *Der Standard*, a newspaper whose pale orange colour made it seem as if the pages had yellowed and aged before you even touched them, and which, given the world news – Iraq, Israel, Zimbabwe – produced in him an anachronistic confusion that seemed to go wonderfully well with the furniture and the gentle hum of voices: a Central European buzz in which people such as Kafka, Schnitzler, Karl Kraus and Heimito von Doderer had so comfortably been able to do their thinking. Perhaps Austria had deliberately chosen to lag behind the times, he thought, because the world was going much too fast. He ordered a second cup of coffee.

The king of procrastination. That's what Anja called him.

'Do you have any idea what you do? You circle around your desk, as far from it as possible, taking hours to reach your computer. As if you're waiting for something to happen, so you can get out of doing whatever it is you're supposed to be doing.'

'But in the meantime I'm thinking.'

'Of course you are. About an even better way to ruin someone's reputation.'

It was not true, but how could you explain that? Most of what was being published was simply not good enough. New writers were appearing every day, and yet if you looked back at the twentieth century, how many real writers had withstood the test of time? So many of the trashy books that were published began to moulder while still on the best-seller lists.

'Your standards are too high,' she said just before he left, and there had been a trace of pity in her voice, or even, God forbid, motherly love. 'Promise me one thing. Forget about all of this once you're there. If it's the waste of time you say it is, there's no point in getting worked up about it. Remember your blood pressure! You're not a twelve-year-old any more.'

He had been hearing that last sentence all too often lately. He had no idea why she had picked the number twelve, rather than twenty-four, or thirty-two, neither of which he was of course, though perhaps, to her, twelve seemed light years away. His blood pressure *was* too high – that was true. And he did have arthritis, and several more of those insidious ailments that made life unpleasant for a person in his late forties – intimations of greater calamìties to come. He had caught himself calculating the average age of death in the obituary columns. It was good when there was an outbreak of salmonella in a nursing home, but bad when three drunk or stoned teenagers, in the grip of an overpowering death wish, came out of a disco and drove straight into a wall and thence into eternity. But he was supposed to forget all of that. 'Otherwise you might as well chuck the money into a canal.' It was expensive, all right. Especially if, as Arnold claimed, they gave you next to nothing to eat.

4

THE BLUE TRAIN TURNED OUT TO BE A TRAM THAT RAN
once an hour. Within minutes they had left Innsbruck behind
and were passing through a snow-covered forest. 'White
soot, cut feathers,' Constantijn Huygens once wrote in a
poem about snow, a line that Erik Zondag now repeated to
himself. No one had ever described snow so beautifully. The
Dutch, who were quick to point to the greatness of
Shakespeare or Racine, were usually incapable of quoting
even one line of Brederode, Hooft or Huygens. A few lines
of Cats and Vondel and that one line of Gorter's had left
their mark on the language, not to mention 'Oh land of
dung and mist', but that was about it for the Dutch classics.

The snow glittered. The gloominess that he had been
carrying around with him ever since he left Amsterdam fell
away. Trees, houses, fields — all buried beneath those cut
feathers. There were only two other passengers left when
he got out at the tiny station of Igls, which was also the
end of the line. A church, and frescoes of saints on the
rustic houses, whose upper storeys of unpainted wood had

retained their original use as haylofts and barns. A sign, with 'Alpenhof' in hand-painted Gothic letters, pointed him towards the road, up a fairly steep incline. He slipped and slid so much in his city shoes that it was all he could do to stay on his feet. Huffing and puffing at the top, he saw before him an austere L-shaped building with a natural-stone exterior and extensive grounds, now blanketed in snow. The car park in the front was filled up with BMWs, Jaguars and Volvos with licence plates from Liechtenstein, Switzerland, Germany and Andorra. Arnold had neglected to mention that. He had talked about how nice the people were, and how being in the same boat had helped them to bond. 'Besides which, a bit of *connaissance du monde* might be helpful, Erik. After twenty years in the rarefied atmosphere of the literary supplement, a bit of oxygen might do you some good.'

Through the glass doors he could see people walking about in white bathrobes. This was his last chance to turn round and run.

'Coward.'

'Yes, Anja.'

He went in. A woman his age was seated at a reception desk. If her tan was anything to go by, she must have flown in three minutes ago from Tenerife, where she would have spent hours every day under a grill. Frau Dr Nicklaus. He told her his name, which she immediately translated into German.

'Herr Sontag! *Herzlich wilkommen!*' She made it sound as if she had been looking forward to his arrival for days. The first step, she explained, was to be introduced to Renate, the woman in charge of the dining room. Renate had also been looking forward to his arrival. While she did not actually smother him with kisses, she did clutch him in a kind of embrace, as if they were about to launch into a waltz, and led him to a table for two by the window which, she informed him, he would be sharing for the rest of the week with Herr Dr Krüger from Regensburg. He had no objection, surely?

'*Ja, ja*, Herr Sontag, and since you're Dutch, I've given you a table with a view of the mountains because I know there aren't any mountains in your country. Officially, your stay here begins tomorrow morning, so you can either eat in the dining room tonight or go down to the village for one last meal before your diet begins. It's up to you.'

He opted for the village. He unpacked his suitcase and arranged his books as he invariably did, delighted finally to be able to read something of his own choosing, and then took a short nap before walking back down to the village. In the Goldene Gans he ordered goose, to honour the restaurant's name, and drank a heavy Austrian wine. It started snowing on his way back, big fat flakes that swirled about him so hard he could scarcely see the road. The *Blauer Burgunder* had given way to a glass of *Himbeergeist* – and then another glass. After all, you were supposed to go all out on your last meal. In bed he tried to read the book that Frau Nicklaus had given him, but gave up when he got to the words of Maimonides: 'Copious meals work on the body like poison and are the primary cause of illness ...' That did not go down well with the goose, and certainly not with the wine and the *Himbeergeist*. He discovered that he had committed his first mortal sin by eating shortly before bedtime, got hopelessly lost in statistics about potassium, magnesium and calcium, decided not to get up in time for the morning exercises in the forest, and at last abandoned himself to the merciful darkness ...

5

. . . IN WHICH ALL KINDS OF THINGS HAPPENED, THOUGH we know more about that than he does. No lowlander can sleep with impunity in the high mountains. The window, which has been left slightly ajar, lets in the cold night air. The man in the bed works his way through a series of dreams, none of which he will remember. In the silence, which he does not notice, an owl hunts its prey and a startled deer plunges into the black syntax of the forest, where Erik Zondag will take a walk tomorrow without identifying the deer's tracks. When he wakes, he will see a snowy mountain range lit by the first rays of the sun — a row of sharp, gleaming-white teeth, daubed here and there with blood.

Herr Dr Krüger — dressed, like Erik, in a white bathrobe — was already sitting at their table when he arrived in the dining room. There was a single bread roll on the plate, and next to that a tiny pitcher with a gooey yellow substance. Erik stared at it helplessly, and then at Herr Dr Krüger, who immediately introduced himself: two gentlemen in bathrobes shaking hands. Krüger was tall, and gave the appearance of not having skipped the morning exercises in the forest (true) and as if, like Ernst Jünger, he took a cold shower every morning, in the hope that, as his shining example, he would live to be a hundred. 'Ach, Holland,' Krüger said, then proceeded to tell him that his car had been broken into once in Amsterdam, that he was a gynaecologist, that he came to the Alpenhof for two weeks every year and always felt rejuvenated afterwards, and that Erik should cut that dry and rather stale-looking bread roll on his plate into thin slices, which was not as easy as it sounded because the bread began to tear. The yellow goo was linseed oil, which he was supposed to dribble on to every slice, since it would lower your cholesterol. Coffee and tea – real tea – were off-limits. The only teas served here were lemon balm or rosemary or some other medicinal witches' brew that you were allowed to drink only twenty minutes after breakfast. 'And don't forget,' Herr Krüger said, 'to chew every bite twenty times.' Erik looked around the room. The woman at the next table was sitting up so straight that he would be willing to bet she had been taking ballet lessons since the day she was born. She stared into space, no doubt counting the bites.

'*Guten Morgen*, Herr Sontag! Did you sleep well? What would you like on your roll?'

Immediately he lost count.

'You have a choice,' Herr Krüger said. 'Either sheep's

milk yogurt or goat's milk cottage cheese with chives.' A few minutes later the waitress brought him a bowl of sheep's milk yogurt. Krüger explained that he was now being put on a mild deprivation diet.

'We all eat too much! Look around you, especially at the shape of people's abdomens – they tell the real story!' As he spoke, he peered over the edge of the table at Erik's abdomen. 'Humph.' It was evidently not as bad as it might have been. 'People always look at themselves in the mirror face on so they don't have to see their paunches, but if they were to look at themselves in profile, they'd see bulging tummies, pot bellies, beer guts – real monstrosities. You'll see what I mean when you go to the sauna or the swimming pool. That's why this is such a good diet. No raw vegetables! No beans! No cabbage, no onions, no garlic! No pork fat – and that means no sausages – and no refined cooking oils! Only easily digested grains and dairy products. Everything has been calculated with ruthless precision in terms of digestibility, because that is the key to good health. Don't think of a human being as an animal, rather as a plant! A plant with a root system! Just as the aerial roots of a plant absorb the nutrients in the soil, the intestinal villi extract the nutrients from the food in the digestive tract and pass them on to the organism's blood and cells! But if you'll excuse me, it's time for my Kneipp cure.' Herr Krüger bowed slightly and strode off, leaving Erik in a state of confusion. He had never given a moment's thought to his digestive tract, and knew as little about the functioning of his body as he did about his computer or his Volvo. Blood was just something you had, and if you were lucky it stayed inside your body while your heart pumped it around, which in his case it had been doing for almost fifty years. 'You're still living in the age before Vesalius,' his doctor had once said to him. 'When the body was yet a mystery.' That was when he had first prescribed pills to lower Erik's cholesterol level and bring down his too-high blood pressure.

'But I feel fine.'

'I know, but you're not. That's why heart disease is known as the silent killer. The combination of these two factors puts you in the danger zone. Follow my instructions, and you'll be all right.'

Renate materialised at his table.

'You do know that they're expecting you downstairs, don't you? Your first appointment is with Sibille, who will measure your blood pressure and take a blood sample. Then you're scheduled for a hay bath.'

He hurried down the slate stairs to a small room, where several other guests were waiting to be summoned. Across from it was a room – as white as the snow outside – where two young women in white were at work at gleaming white desks. He listened to the people around him, who were speaking German and Russian, along with the strange variants of German that he liked to think had been shaped by high mountains and deep valleys: Swiss German, Austrian

– languages he associated with air-dried beef and unusual types of cheese. It was not an unpleasant wait.

'Herr Sontag?' Another figure in white. Sibille. She had one wall eye and moved as if she were weightless. He was aware that they had shaken hands, but he had not felt a thing. The same could be said of the blood sample. Sibille was a star with a needle. He watched the vial fill with blood and tried, not very successfully, to think of something else. 'You'll see,' Arnold had said. 'After two days you'll surrender altogether. You'll be like putty in their hands.' It was true. The wall-eyed creature floated weightlessly ahead of him as though they were inside a spaceship, pulled aside a curtain, told him to take off all his clothes, held up a sheet of transparent plastic for him to see, spread it over a bed, and instructed him to lie down upon it. He tried to make contact with the good eye so he could tell what was going to happen next, but she had already pressed a button, and a moment later he found himself inside a womb, in which the amniotic fluid, smelling strongly of hay, sloshed wildly up and down before finally coming to rest. In her mountain dialect, the Sibille butterfly told him when she would be back, but he felt himself sinking into a state of deep relaxation and accepted that, at least for the time being, he had no desire to be born.

'You'd really like to stay in there, wouldn't you?' said Sibille the midwife when she woke him out of his dream of barnyards, heifers and haystacks. She handed him a towel and led him into a larger room, where an elderly lady, lifting her feet as high as possible, was walking through a pond, filled with pebbles. The idea, Sibille said, was for him to pick his way across the pond like a heron, just as the lady was doing. First you had to dip your feet in a wooden tub filled with hot water, and then walk across the pebbles. It was good for your circulation. Scarcely was he out of the womb, and already the suffering had begun. The pond water had been flown in specially from Spitsbergen, and the sharp pebbles hurt his feet. Clutching the hem of his robe, he tried to step like a stork, and imagined what his colleagues at the paper would say if only they could see him now. He read a cryptic motto on the wall, something to the effect that 'you are who you are where you are who you are', and listened to a discussion about traditional Chinese medicine, in which the fifth season, late summer, is also the season of the earth. 'In the Fire element,' a voice explained, as he dipped his feet into the hot water again, 'man reaches the fullness of his "I", but in the autumn the Earth element comes into play, going from the safe "I" to the risky "you". It takes courage to do that – the courage to connect to others, to grow towards the earth. Connections, connective tissue, the infrastructure connecting everything in our bodies . . .' He lost the thread of the monologue, vaguely heard the words 'spleen' and 'pancreas', wondered whether these organs could also be found in *his* body, did another round in the icy water, then fled to his room – the Heather

Rose room. On the way he passed Larkspur, Goldenrod and Columbine, before reaching the fitness room, where slaves were working out on torture machines. One young woman was running a Sisyphus-like race on a rubber belt that kept rolling round and round, the Russian from the waiting room was trying to lift a massive set of weights on a pulley from a sitting position, and another victim, with a bright red face and a strap around his hips was fighting gravity as he tried to raise himself. All that labour, he thought, and not a single product to show for it. Later it occurred to him that he had never been so aware of his body. He was incessantly reminded of it, as it was smeared with oil, massaged, rubbed with salt, put into a bath filled with mud and hay, and fed a measly roll in the morning and a minimalist composition in the afternoon, on which the painter/ sculptor had clearly lavished great attention, though every last calorie had no doubt been burned up by the time he had finished the first mile of his daily walk. In the evenings he was allowed to choose between a bread roll and a potato – a lonely tuber whose elongated shape made it look more substantial than the roll – lying in the middle of his plate, dreaming of a juicy pork chop that would never come. The thick drops of cold linseed oil that he dribbled onto the lonely potato by way of compensation reminded him of the cod liver oil he had been forced to swallow as a child. On top of that they were served two heaped teaspoons of salmon mousse or avocado mush – company for the long night ahead, in which the only thing to happen was the consumption of a white powder dissolved in a glass of water, just as every day began with a bitter brew that a few hours later set off an internal cataclysm not unlike volcanic eruptions and mudslides that wiped out entire villages and killed thousands.

He no longer knew what to think of it all. If someone had told him he would have to spend the rest of his life with Herr Dr Krüger, he would not have batted an eyelid. Dutch literature, the paper, the approaching war, even Anja – everything had sunk to the depths of his consciousness. He slept like a log, and noticed to his amazement that he had no desire for sex or booze, that he looked forward to his vegetable bouillon – for which they all lined up daily at quarter to eleven – and also to Sibille's massage. When he finally got up enough courage to tell her that he had never come across a woman with such strong fingers, a woman who (though he did not dare to add this part) looked like a pixie whose weight could hardly be registered on an earthly scale, she replied that she owed her strength to being a mountain climber, so that he had visions of those same ten fingers clutching the jagged edge of a cliff as she dangled above a yawning abyss.

6

WE WILL LEAVE HIM NOW TO FEND FOR HIMSELF IN HIS
new universe of dietary laws and virtuous digestion, of
monastic hours and herbal tea. He will never again be able
to eat raw vegetables in the evening without a pang of guilt,
he can feel an ocean of herbal tea sloshing around inside
him, and he cannot imagine what his days would be like
without Herr Dr Krüger – who has explained the secrets
of Chinese medicine to him – or without the two charming
lesbians at the next table, or without the sausage manu-
facturer from Liechtenstein who swims with him in the
Olympic-sized pool, or without aqua fitness and qigong.
The list of things he is not allowed to eat, drink or do
grows day by day. Sometimes he has the feeling that he is
wresting a new body out of his old one, which he can
either leave behind in the Alpenhof, like a pile of dirty
laundry, or else donate to a medical school for dissection.
He does not know exactly what he is going to do with the
new one, except that he is not going to pollute it with
coffee or alcohol. This new body belongs to a saint with a

transparent digestive tract and the heart and liver of a twenty-year-old Tibetan nun.

In the afternoon he goes for a walk in the mountains, hiking a bit further each day through a forest of tall, snow-tipped firs. One day he walks to Patsch and Heiligwasser, calling out '*Grüss Gott*' to every hiker he meets. This, he thinks, is what Death must feel like – euphoria at being cut off from your previous life, free at last! Along the path he habitually takes, simple souls have depicted Christ's suffering, painting the Stations of the Cross on little wayside altars, mounted on wooden posts and placed a couple of hundred yards apart. Only on the fifth day does he have enough breath to climb to the Resurrection. White sunlight filters down through the trees, and the transparent shaft of light seems to beam directly at him. All that is lacking is a gold frame big enough to hold the image.

7

THINGS CAN'T GO ON LIKE THIS. IT IS TIME TO BRING him down to earth.

Upon his return to the Alpenhof, he finds a note in his pigeonhole, informing him that Sibille has had a minor accident in the climbing school, so that someone else will be massaging him tomorrow, and a letter addressed to him in Anja's impetuous handwriting, which he does not bother to open. Back in his room he watches the lights in the village go on one by one, listens to the bells record the angelus, and reflects on the fact that he has no desire to return to his recent past, though what he does not realise is that lurking beneath that past is another past, which has been dormant for the last three years – biding its time in the guise of an angel – and which at this very moment is preparing to take him back to that earlier time, there where he never wanted to be again.

We grant him a night of what he supposes is dreamless sleep. Towards morning a storm comes up and blows the snow in all directions. He gets up later than usual, drinks his *Bitterwasser*, eats his *Semmelbrötchen* at the unexpectedly empty table, and watches Herr Dr Krüger fighting his way through the blizzard like a cinema version of Amundsen, then goes downstairs to wait in the room where Sibille usually comes to collect him. What happens next is, grammatically speaking, not easy to say. 'They take each other's breath away' comes the closest to it, but since we already know him and do not expect to find her here, that will not get us very far. They have met before – that much is clear. What no one can see, however, are the wings he mentally attaches to her back, the wings of an angel he has never been able to forget. Before he can say a word, she puts the forefinger of her left hand to her lips and pulls him to his feet with her right hand. 'Herr Zondag,' she says, pronouncing his name correctly and free of any accent, then asks him to follow her to the massage room, into both the future and the past, which requires such opposing movements that his body reacts with a single spasmodic jerk. The last that we see are the strange contortions of a man standing in front of a poster with illustrations of foot reflexes and acupuncture points, a man about to attempt to lift a boulder that is much too heavy for him.

8

ANGELS DO NOT EXIST, AND YET THEY ARE DIVIDED INTO orders, much like the hierarchy in an army. They fly to and fro in frescoes, act as the bearers of glad tidings in the paintings of Raphael and Giotto, serve as stone guardians by the graves of the rich in Buenos Aires and Genoa, and accompany the doomed to the outer gates of Paradise with their flaming swords held high. They have names, bodies and wings; they are genderless and yet they are not women; they are immortal, which means that no skeletal remains have ever been found, so that no one has ever been able to examine them to find out how those gigantic wings are connected to their shoulder blades — in short, they are part of the world around us even though they do not exist, and yet the last time Erik had seen the short, slender woman now standing before him in a spa in Austria, she had had two large grey wings with a silvery sheen. During that first encounter, he had not seen her face, because she had been curled up in a cupboard with her back to him, nor would he succeed in seeing it now, because she ordered him, in the tone used by masseuses the world over, to lie down on his stomach. He did as he was told. He could feel his heart beating wildly, just as he could feel her hands trembling, the same hands that had touched his body for the last time three years ago. That had been in Perth, in Western Australia, thousands of miles from Sydney, on the opposite shore of the continent. She said not a word. Not then, and not now. The years in between had been sucked away with a violence that made his head spin. He took hold of the massage table with both hands.

'Don't tense up like that.' The well-remembered, rather husky voice — as bewitching as ever — spoke softly in an accent that had puzzled him the first time he had heard it. He began to reply, but since he was lying face down and a towel was draped loosely over the table, it came out sounding more like a sob. She laid her hand on his head for a moment, which only made it worse. Suddenly, all of the sadness which he had disguised so well that he had been able to pretend it had gone away came back to him now with such force that he felt as if a bandage had been yanked viciously from a wound. He started to raise his head so that he could look at her, but she pressed it firmly down again. 'Later,' she said. 'Later.' And as if it were a magic word, he felt his body relax, felt the lost time flowing back to him, felt himself being enveloped again in the madness of their tale — which had been perfectly logical despite the madness. He wanted to fire off a thousand questions, but he knew this was not the right time. He was the only man who had ever been embraced by an angel. Even now he could feel how she had enfolded him in the wings that she no longer had, and during the massage — no, even before that — he surrendered himself to his memories with such ease that he seemed to be stealing back to the past, to seek refuge there. Who knows, he might even have fallen asleep.

9

IT HAD BEEN SUMMER WHEN HE ARRIVED IN PERTH. HE had never been cooped up in a plane for so long. The eighteen hours to Sydney had been followed by a flight across a continent with a population only slightly larger than that of the Netherlands, though it was nearly as big as the United States. Much of the land was empty: a rocky, sunburnt, sand-coloured desert, where the Aborigines had led their unwatched, autonomous lives for thousands of years. The others – the sheep ranchers and the winegrowers – lived on the periphery.

He had been invited to Perth for a literary festival, which, for a change, was not just for writers and poets, but also for translators, publishers and critics – the whole parasitical or gritty underlayer that revolved around the lonely core of a book or a poem in a relationship of mutual dependence that was sometimes fruitful and sometimes disgusting. He loathed most writers as people, especially those whose work he admired. It was better not to meet them at all. Writers were supposed to lead a paper existence — between the covers of a book. You should not have to be distracted by body odours, awful haircuts, bizarre footwear, unsuitable spouses, needless gossip, professional jealousy, whorish behaviour, coquetry or boastfulness. The plenary sessions were held in tents; it was summertime in March, with temperatures well over a hundred degrees. He found himself on a panel with a Tasmanian poet, a literary editor at the *Neue Zürcher Zeitung*, a novelist from Queensland and a publisher from Sydney. Their wisdoms burbled over the heads of the audience, which consisted mostly of middle-aged women. He noticed that many of his points of reference were not valid here. The importance of the difference in outlook between the two major Dutch newspapers had begun to fade by Dunkirk and Düsseldorf, and at greater distances most of the topics hotly debated among insiders in his now so faraway country were about as scintillating as an obscure tribal war in Swaziland or a theological dispute in the Middle Ages. After the panel discussion, the novelist and the poet signed books at a table set up outside the tent, but since publishers and critics do not normally have anything to sign, he and the publisher, along with the literary editor and a Danish writer who had been in the audience, sat down on a patch of grass with a bottle of wine and four glasses. Erik Zondag soon lost interest in the conversation. While the editor and the publisher rambled on about print runs, best-seller lists, advertising and the connection between them, he listened to the histrionic cries of an Indonesian poet, which could be heard coming from one of the tents, watched the evening slide with tropical torpor between the spreading trees, and wondered if he ever wanted to go home again. After his divorce, he had been on his own for a while – a time of brief affairs, bar-room friendships and attempts to write poetry, which he later rightly tore up. It was after that – too soon, he now understood – that he had met Anja. He had made quite a name for himself by taking potshots at a few literary giants, so the newspaper for which he still worked had offered him a permanent position. He was exactly what they were looking for: someone to 'raise hell and shake things up'. The literary pond was cluttered with too many ducks and swans, and it was necessary to cull them from time to time. Literature had become a career. Every numbskull who had with gathering distaste studied Dutch literature felt the need to write a novel, which meant that masterly debuts were following on the heels of one another more rapidly than ever. He was part of the clean-up crew. It was a nasty job, but useful. The times he had been able genuinely to wax lyrical about a book had been glorious exceptions. All that mediocrity week after week seemed to cling to his hair and creep under his nails. Besides, the work itself had been a bitter disappointment. The books he really wanted to review were usually assigned to a man with a turgid style – a dyed-in-the-wool Catholic who would have been better off teaching at a school somewhere in the provinces. The man had a preference for authors such as Jünger and Bataille, but had never written an original word about one of the writers and thinkers he was forever reviewing. His reviews were echoes of things he had read elsewhere, and yet the editor-in-chief had lured him away from Anja's paper purely on the strength of those big-name authors he reviewed, because even though no one read his dull and excruciatingly long essays, a newspaper with any pretensions at all had to have a philosopher on its staff. To make matters worse, in some bewildering way the man always seemed to miss the point – an intellectual colour-blindness or lack of instinct or intuition that no one else seemed to notice. When the first – and also the best – of the so-called Three Great Writers in Dutch literature set off on his journey towards posthumous publication, the man had immediately proclaimed another triumvirate, prompted no doubt by his Catholic instinct for hierarchy. Judging by the conversation going on around him, things were no different here, although Australian writers were separated by blissfully vast distances, which must cut down on the jealousy, inbreeding and backbiting. The best solution, he thought, would be to live in an abandoned house on a rocky northern shore, where a winged messenger came once a week to deliver a book that you could really sink your teeth into. At least you would not run across a review in which someone ridiculed a poet because she dared to use a fancy word like 'rhetoric' in one of her poems. 'Base-born products of base beds,' Yeats had called the new Neanderthalers. But Anja had warned him not to get upset.

'What you haven't grasped is that there's a new generation of writers,' she said. 'They're used to a fast pace. They're not interested in those cobwebs of yours. These days it's all about plots, madness and humour, not grandiose speculations, philosophical drivel and intellectual posturing.'

But it was too late to learn Norwegian or emigrate to Australia. He'd have to go on writing for the literary supplement until he died, unless they fired him for not keeping up with the spirit of the times, or until the paper itself was sold, and that was also a possibility.

He was startled out of his reverie by hearing one of the men beside him say the word 'angel' in a thick German accent: 'Zer are an-chels all over zis city. Zey are *ev*-ry-vere!'

'Yes, I've seen them,' the publisher said. 'A fantastic idea! I did the tour yesterday.'

Erik remembered reading about this tour and immediately dismissing it as a waste of time. Considering the publisher's enthusiasm, however, he had apparently been mistaken. In addition to the literary festival, there was a theatre and ballet festival, and angels had something to do with that. He had seen a picture in the *Australian* of a life-sized angel with a sword, poised atop a department store or a multi-storey car park, and wondered if it had been an actual person or a statue, like the one on the roof of the insurance company on the Singel Canal in Amsterdam, not far from where he lived.

'No,' the poet said, 'this one was real. I saw it too, because it moved. Oddly enough, I had a hard time spotting her — at any rate, I'm pretty sure it was a she, because I had my binoculars with me. Here, you can have my booklet, I won't be needing it any more. The whole tour takes a few hours.' He reached into his bag, rummaged through the muddle of poems he had used for his reading, then handed him a spiral-bound booklet with narrow plastic pages. When you joined them up, they charted the route of a maze-like treasure hunt through Perth, with detailed directions and photographs of buildings. It opened with a quote from Rilke: 'Angels, it is said, are often unsure whether they pass among the living or the dead.' The next quote had been taken from *Paradise Lost*:

> *In either hand the hast'ning Angel caught*
> *Our ling'ring Parents . . .*

Adam and Eve. He had never thought of them as parents, if only because they were generally depicted in the nude, with just a fig leaf. And angels? When was the last time he had thought about angels, he asked himself, or had he never really thought about them because they had been so much a part of his childhood? You saw them everywhere in those days, in prayer books and stained-glass windows. If you were a Catholic, you could not avoid them. Even Lucifer was a fallen angel. And if all was well, you had a guardian angel watching over you. There were various types of angels, all of which you had to learn: seraphim and cherubim, thrones and powers. For some inexplicable reason angels never seemed to grow old (a middle-aged angel was inconceivable!), they had 'locks' rather than hair, their feet were always bare, and of course they never wore glasses. There is a moment in which something that appears to be quite ordinary suddenly becomes mysterious. So while he wondered what an angel would look like in full flight and how much air would be displaced by the wings – mysteries in both the sacred and the aerodynamic sense – he decided to go to the festival office and sign up for the 'angel hunt', because, as he now realised, that was what it boiled down to. Angels had been hidden in various places throughout the city, and the idea was for you to find as many of them as possible. All you had to do was to show up at a specific time, promise to go on your own, and let yourself be taken to the starting point by someone who had been instructed not to answer any questions.

10

PERTH IS IN SOUTHWEST AUSTRALIA. THE NEAREST STATE capital is Adelaide, about 1,200 miles to the east as the crow flies. If you do not want to take a plane, you have to drive along the coast or through a broiling desert. Sydney, Melbourne and Brisbane are a continent away, which makes Perth an exception in more ways than one: it is the capital of Western Australia, though it does not quite fit in with the rest of the state; it is located on the Swan River, which curves sensuously before flowing into the Indian Ocean; it has made a half-hearted attempt to resemble a real city by erecting a few skyscrapers; and it is a mixture of England and the tropics, with many public parks and suburbs, with lots of low houses and gardens full of flowers – all very welcome in a hot climate that slows the pace. In short, thought Erik Zondag, it is the very last place you would expect to find angels in the early years of the new millennium, though that was hardly a reason not to go looking for them. Who knows, he might even get a good story out of it for the paper. According to the instructions, he was to report to the tenth level of Wilson's Car Park on Hay Street at 2.40 p.m. High-rise car parks were not his favourite architectural structures. Although it was nearly April, it was high summer and sweltering hot as he stood on the roof, scanning Perth stretched out below him, and the Swan River disappearing with a glitter of sunlight into the infinity of the ocean. It was here that Dutch traders had first clapped eyes on this continent, only to turn up their noses when they found nothing of value. No gold, no nutmeg — just weird furry animals that leaped instead of walked and natives that were nothing like the ones they had been dreaming of.

On the tenth level he encountered a young man who seemed to be expecting him. 'Mr Sundag?'

'Yes?'

'Here's a copy of the booklet, showing you the route you need to follow. This gentleman here will drive you to Barrack's Arch, which is the actual starting point. The whole thing will take about three hours, and at the end the route will lead you back here.' He sat in silence beside the stranger, who drove him to a brick building, where another silent man opened the door for him and then left him on his own. A dusty stairwell, a heap of rubbish on the landing, dry eucalyptus leaves blown in by the wind, old newspapers, steps painted a reddish brown. Silence. An empty room, an open sleeping bag, a couple of snapshots on a windowsill. Was this supposed to mean something?

Was he following a trail? An indistinct map – not of any place he recognised, aerial photographs, spider webs. The roar of the nearby highway. There were six lanes here. Where did all those cars come from? Perth was not *that* big. He could hear the sound of his own footsteps. There was not an angel anywhere to be seen. He had obviously missed whatever it was he was supposed to see. Maybe it was all a stupid joke. He felt somewhat uncomfortable, and also tired, as if that endless flight was still playing havoc with his body. Why had he agreed to this nonsense? According to the booklet, when he emerged from Barrack's Arch he was to turn left and walk down the hill to 240 St George's Terrace. He walked as he normally would – a mere pedestrian among other pedestrians. They cannot see what I am up to, he thought. I am looking for angels, but they do not know that, and if I were to tell them, they would think I was crazy. That last part appealed to him. He found himself noticing things he would not usually have noticed. After all, anything might be a clue, a key, an allusion. Then he found himself in a bare room with just a few scribbled messages: *Anne, which corner are you on? Etiam ne nescis?* After that another heap of dusty leaves, spokes without a wheel, an entryway, a closed steel door, and then, suddenly, hanging on a railing, a few lines of *Paradise Lost* – the ones in which Adam and Eve, evicted from Paradise by a heavenly bouncer with wings, turn back for one last look:

In either hand the hast'ning Angel caught
Our ling'ring parents, and to th' Eastern Gate
Led them direct, and down the Cliff as fast
To the subjected Plaine; then disappeer'd.

And it was true. Before him lay a sorry patch of no-man's-land: a rusty refrigerator, dead twigs, sand, weeds, a bare concrete wall. Behind him things were not much better: an empty lift shaft, disconnected electrical wires leading nowhere since the power had long since been shut off, and not an angel in sight. Here Paradise had been lost for good. If they were hoping to evoke a feeling of despair, it had worked. Erik caught himself thinking of original sin, confessionals and the musty smell that goes with them. Stale cigar smoke coming out of shadowy mouths which you could barely see in the semi-darkness, speaking of sin and penance.

No, these are not agreeable thoughts. Feeling as if he is being watched, he checks the walls for a hidden camera, but does not see one. The choice is clear: he can either give up right now or go on to the next clue. *Go to the Paragon foyer, take the lift to level 5 and walk up the stairs to level 6.* An empty office suite, dust on the floor, a long row of metal filing cabinets. According to his count, there are twenty-nine of them. The rest of the space is empty, apart from two birdcages, each with two birds. A torn label attached to one of the cages turns out to be blank. Erik and the birds stare at each other, the way people and animals do — a meaningless gaze across an unbridgeable distance. He goes out again, passing through what was once a kitchen, climbs up a flight of metal stairs, listens to his ringing footsteps, and finds himself in another vacant office. Instead of filing cabinets, this one has a huge metal bin filled with books. The titles all have something to do with God or saints — Anglican life in an earlier era. A bit further away is another bin, this one filled with white feathers (angels have to start somewhere, after all), as if someone had given a good shake to a pillow full of cherubs. As he flees the building, a man thrusts a note into his hand: *On your way to Bank West, please stop at the Hay Street Shop, between the Croissant Express and the Educina Café.* He follows the directions. His hotel cannot be far off, he thinks, though everything looks different now. He does not want to become an ordinary pedestrian, but he catches sight of himself on a surveillance monitor and is unpleasantly surprised. The fruit has apparently already been plucked from the Tree of the Knowledge of Good and Evil, because there is a box of apples on the pavement. *Take an apple.*

It is cool inside the Bank West building, with the sudden chill of air conditioning in the tropics. A girl in blue stands up and all but takes him by the hand. In the lift she presses 46. The white-shirted office-workers who get in as the lift makes its way up have nothing to do with the angel hunt, but when he reaches the forty-sixth floor, another white-shirted man gets up from his desk, opens a door for him, then closes it behind him, so that he finds himself alone in an executive suite, listening to a fax machine regurgitate reams of white paper. He picks up one of the sheets and sees two dozen lines from *Paradise Lost*. On the desk are file folders about various projects. The text on the computer screen changes to read: '. . . if you will come I will put out fresh pillows for you. This room and this springtime contain only you,' then switches over to the hierarchy in the kingdom of angels: Archangels, Powers, Virtues. 'Come soon, Death is demanding: we have much to atone for, before little by little we begin to taste of Eternity. In a bed of roses the Seraphim slumber . . .' Still not craving eternity, he stands by the window and stares down at the streams and streams of cars on the highway. As he leaves the room, he bumps into the Danish writer. Surely that cannot be part of the plan? They exchange guilty looks, then simultaneously raise their fingers to their lips. Later on, he sees a girl in a tight grey skirt. Is she an angel? She avoids his glance, struts around as if she owns the place, looks out towards the hills and the faraway ocean, and plays with the plastic water bottle in her hands. Once again, he is struck by the absurdity of the whole thing. Why is he here? What is he doing in a vacant office suite that has in it only a couple of flowerpots filled with primroses? Is he inspecting the available property? But now that he has begun, he does not want to stop. Then at last his perseverance pays off: in the small, nondescript church that he has passed each day, he sees his first real angels – two men, sitting a couple of feet apart in the choir stalls. They are clearly flesh and blood, but they do have wings. He sits in the muted light poring in through the stained-glass windows and stares at the angels. They stare back at him. No one says a word. The angels rearrange their wings, the way swans and sparrows do. After a while he leaves the church and turns into a narrow side street that leads to a courtyard, which is piled high with rubbish bins. And then he spots his third angel: a man with close-cropped hair sitting behind a chain-link fence, a heavenly prisoner in a cage filled with cardboard boxes. He starts to go over to him, but then catches sight of the Tasmanian poet – taking the tour for the second time, apparently – standing on the other side of the cage and gazing lustfully at the angel, as if to elicit a promise. The moment the poet leaves, the angel relaxes his stare. He is sitting on his heels, and as Erik approaches, there is another silent vis-à-vis, even worse than with the birds. After that, there is a rapid succession of angels. He follows the invisible threads that have been laid for him, goes in and out of buildings, sees a paralysed angel in a wheelchair with his wings draped over the armrests, almost trips over a man lying on the floor, his bare feet crossed disarmingly at the ankles and his white wings stretched out on a dirty grey carpet, then two black women in a window seat who smile at him, but do not speak. Clues and messages are being thrust at him all the time: *I am deeply sorry for any pain you may be feeling. Please call.* Call who? At what number? The message is about as meaningful as the other objects in the room: an open drawer full of feathers, a yellowed copy of the *West Australian*, the score of Ethelbert Nevin's 'Rosary', white grains of salt scattered across a roof. Later he would come to believe that this series of increasingly outlandish absurdities had inevitably led to that one small room, where the woman who was massaging him now had then been lying in a cupboard with her face turned to the wall. Even at the time he knew it was a moment he would never forget. A flight of unpainted stairs that kept going up and up until eventually he reached an empty floor, and then a room with dirty windows, through which he could just make out the grey outlines of the skyscrapers, and at last, curled up in the cupboard, that small body, half hidden by a pair of grey wings. For a moment he thought it was a boy or a young child. He stared at the wings. They had been made out of real feathers and put together so cleverly that it was almost creepy. Who knows, maybe this woman could indeed fly. He caught a glimpse of black hair and light brown skin. He could hear her breathing. She had not moved a muscle, and yet she knew that someone was in the room.

11

SHE TAPS HIM GENTLY ON THE SHOULDER AND ASKS HIM to turn over. For one split second he is still there, in the past, back in that little room. He turns to lie on his back, though he is not ready to look at her face, if only because he had not been able to see it then either. 'Tell me what it felt like,' he says.

'You know what it felt like.'

'Perhaps, but tell me anyway.'

'You weren't the only person who stood there for a long time. We had been trained to deal with that kind of situation. To us it was just a role. And yet there was an irresistible pull – on both sides – that you were supposed to resist. Except that in your case it was different. I felt the intensity. As if you were looking at me with laser beams. I could also hear you breathing. You coughed once. I recognised the sound the next day when you came back. That's when you reached out and touched me.'

'And you turned over.'

'Yes, but not until later.'

She knows he is dying to ask just one question, but this is not the right moment. She knows all that went on before: the reason for her untouchability, things he cannot possibly know. She had almost been tempted, though she would never tell him why, because it had something to do with compassion, with the things that had happened to her in the weeks before that. He had no way of knowing who she was, and that was fine. She did not know his story either, and that was also fine. As long as things stayed that way.

But what about him? A man standing in a room in Australia, staring at an angel lying on the floor. Angels are mythical creatures. In this day and age, however, they are usually relegated to the realm of kitsch, irony or theatre. And yet that tiny curled-up body, those bare feet, the whole of that womanly being (he was sure it was a woman, despite the boyish appearance), evoked something in him — fear, tenderness, desire — that made him want to see her stand up and spread those wings, now draped so foolishly across the dusty floor. But he did not dare to say a word. Only at the sound of footsteps on the stairs did he steal away. That night he could not sleep. He took part in a debate on the function of criticism, together with a writer from the Solomon Islands ('There's no literary criticism in my country, and the Australians ignore us. The advantage is that no one says anything bad about you; the disadvantage is that you don't exist'), and after that he got drunk with the Danish writer ('The angels are all actors. It's just a game. If you want to see them without their wings, you'll have to go to the bar in the festival building. They all hang out there till late'). And that is exactly what he had done, although he had not seen anyone even remotely resembling her. But how can you recognise a person whose face you have not seen? You have to imagine her without the wings, mentally unbend a curled-up form, set it on its feet — it was impossible.

The next day was the last day of the festival. He jotted down the name of the street and the number of the house and spent the day in a kind of daze, wondering if he would have the courage to go again, as nervous as a teenager. At the end of the day, he climbed the unpainted stairs. She was lying in the same position.

The phrase 'Life is a gamble and an illusion, fraught with risk,' which he had read somewhere, kept running through his head. He no longer remembered who had written it, or even the context in which he had read it, and was not really sure what it meant either. The silence in this house was indeed spooky, but where was the risk? As he stepped into the room, he heard his own footsteps, and she could undoubtedly hear them too. He stared at her motionless body, the bare feet, the wings. What would happen if he said something? It would be like hurling a brick at a mirror, the sound of shattering glass, ugly, a kind of crystal shriek, followed by another silence — a silence that would violate the untouchable. He sat down, leaned back against the wall. Everything — the tension, his feeling that a trap was about to be sprung — had conspired to make time, which is weightless, as heavy as lead. Once he thought he heard someone coming, but it was a false alarm. He brushed her wing with his fingertip, the lightest of touches.

'Please go away.'

'I can't. I want to talk to you.' That was true. He could not leave. Everything about him had become heavier: his body, the discussions he had been having since his arrival in Australia, the flight, the strange city, the new faces, and before that all the rest, his life, his work, Anja, whom he had met after a failed marriage, his unfinished PhD on F. C. Terborgh, still tucked away somewhere in a drawer. An overwhelming desire for sleep came over him. He wished he could lie down, just as she had, on those dirty wooden floorboards in front of the cupboard. Suddenly he no longer cared what might happen. She could dial an alarm number, or else spring to her feet, jump over his outstretched body and race down the stairs. In that case he would follow her and no doubt get himself arrested for assault by the first policeman who answered her call for help.

'Please go away.' Those three simple words hung in the silence as if they were waiting to be sculpted. *Please go away.* An accent. Probably one of the Romance languages, which meant she could be from anywhere. Spain, Romania? No, it was a bit too melodious for that.

Outside, the clock struck six. The festival was officially over. Breathlessly he waited to see if she would move, but she still surprised him. Later he found it impossible to describe how she had managed to sit up so quickly with those wings. It was almost like a spin. In any case she unfurled herself with a corkscrew-like twist, so that in one easy motion she went from lying down to sitting up cross-legged on the floor, with her wings folded behind her. And he knew immediately, with absolute certainty, that he would have waited for days to see that face, even though he would never be able to describe it adequately. It was both open and closed, serene and troubled, defiant and with-drawn. But also full of promise and, as he now understood, now that he was seeing it for the second time, it was like a trap. The grey eyes and the mouth with its slightly parted lips were expectant, mocking.

12

SHE RESTED HER HAND BETWEEN HIS SHOULDER BLADES for a moment, then turned and lifted it in such a way that it felt as if she were scooping something out of his body — pain, exhaustion, sorrow — and releasing it into the air. It is a gesture masseurs sometimes use to indicate that the time is up. He started to sit up, but she stopped him. 'Wait a bit. I've given you a deep massage. I think you might have fallen asleep.'

'How long have you been massaging me?'

'A little over an hour. I didn't have an appointment after yours, so I let you stay longer.'

'And in that time, I've gone back three years. In case you've forgotten, it's been three years exactly since we last met.'

'I haven't forgotten. Of course you're going to ask me why.'

'Why what?'

'Why I disappeared.'

'Why you didn't get in touch with me.'

'I couldn't.'

'Why did you promise me you would?'

'I promised something else as well.'

'What?'

'That I'd see you again.'

'Don't be ridiculous. Running into each other here is pure coincidence, a freak chance. For all I knew, you could have been in Kinshasa. What brought you to this snowy mountaintop anyway? I didn't even know you were a masseuse.'

'I've been doing this for years. I took a course and everything. You can always earn a living at it, whether you're in Austria or Australia. Not every country is like yours, where you can go on the dole when you're out of work.'

'But why here?'

'No particular reason.'

'A man?'

She made a gesture, a flick of the wrist, as if she might be tossing away a theoretical man.

'Where I am has never really mattered to me.'

'So you told me back then: "The world is my home." You know, that really turned me on.' He stood up and grabbed his bathrobe. He wanted to say something, but wasn't sure what. 'I fell madly in love with you.'

'I know, you were pathetically eager.'

'So you were laughing at me?'

'No, just the opposite: I was terrified. It was all happening so fast. There was something frenzied about it.'

'That was because of the party. All I wanted to do at that moment was leave my whole life behind.' And if I had drowned that night, I would not have cared. But he did not tell her that.

'It was because of the wings. You weren't the only one. A lot of weird things happened that last night.'

'No, it wasn't the wings. It had more to do with the fact that it was my last day. My plane was leaving in the morning, and I knew I'd be going back to a life I no longer wanted. And I had the feeling that you understood . . . that you also felt . . .'

He looked at her. He had not been able to read the expression in those cool grey eyes back then either. He had been a fool.

'That I also felt . . .' she repeated, as if she were considering it. She shook her head. 'No,' she said, 'I know myself too well. It wouldn't have worked. You said you wanted to become a foreign correspondent, and when I said that I never stayed in any one place for long, you said you'd go wherever I went, because you could write anywhere. I've heard it all a thousand times. Not those exact words, but still . . . No one can put up with my lifestyle. Besides, I knew you'd go back to your girlfriend and forget me after three months. And I was right.'

'If you were so sure of yourself, why didn't you phone me?'

'Because I didn't want to take the risk.' And then,

abruptly switching the subject, as if to indicate that the conversation was at an end, she said, 'How long will you be staying here?'

'Tomorrow is my last day.'

'That appears to be a speciality of yours.'

'So it would seem. Can we meet somewhere?'

'No,' she said. 'It's against the rules.' She checked her appointment book. 'I've got you down for tomorrow morning, so I'll see you then. Goodbye.'

'Goodbye.'

'Do you remember,' she said at the door, 'the last thing I said to you that night?'

But he did not remember.

13

SINCE IT WAS THEIR LAST EVENING, RENATE GAVE THEM
an extra portion of salmon mousse. Erik chewed his bread
roll down to the last fibre, while Herr Dr Krüger lectured
him on the crueller aspects of ectopic pregnancies: foetal
tissue without a soul but with hair and tiny fingernails. His
mind was on other things. There was a message from Anja,
which he did not feel up to answering. Night was already
starting to swallow the tall white tips of the trees outside
the windows. He wandered through the building, went to
the sauna in the hope that the heat would calm his racing
mind, swam umpteen lengths until he was exhausted, and
went down to the dining room for a cup of bedtime tea,
a bitter brew that was always kept on a sideboard, but when
he finally went to bed, sleep refused to come. If he had
been at home, he would have poured himself a double
brandy, but that was out of the question here. He ran his
tongue over his teeth, trying to rub off the bitter taste of
the graveyard tea, but that did not work either. What she
had said was not true: he had not forgotten her after three

months. Not after three months and not after three years. He had not forgotten her at all, and he never would. Three years ago, after he came back from his trip, he had talked about her so much that he had driven everyone crazy, especially Anja.

'I don't begrudge you your fun. You can screw every one of the heavenly hosts for all I care, but I don't want to hear another word about that angel of yours. If she was so fantastic, you should have stayed there. Who knows, *you* might even have sprouted wings. God, men are pathetic. A woman puts on a pair of wings and curls up in a cupboard. Great. But she still can't fly. And making love with those things on sounds positively uncomfortable. Come to think of it, how did they attach the wings? With elastic straps or what?'

14

THE SAME PLACE, THE SAME CHARACTERS.

Before he lay down on the massage table, he asked her a question he had promised himself he would not ask.

'Are we ever going to see each other again?'

'We've already seen each other again! Have you been able to remember what I said to you at the end of that night?'

No, he still had no idea. The whole of that crazy night – the chaos, the pandemonium – was printed indelibly on his memory: the ocean, the surf, winged people running across the beach, alcohol, sirens, the sinister silhouettes of the ghostly gum trees with their diseased-looking bark.

'Lie down on your stomach, please.' He did as she instructed. But before lowering his mouth to the table, he asked, 'Does massaging me make you feel uncomfortable?'

'God, no. This is my profession. Relax and stop rooting around in the past. Otherwise the massage won't do you any good.'

He saw the scene again, as though it had happened yesterday. A bare room with an empty cupboard. A feather had fallen to the floor, and he picked it up. By then, they had known each other only half an hour. She stood before him, a boyish angel whose face was filled with mockery and suspicion. The phone rang three times in the next room, then stopped. A moment later, it rang again, another three times.

'That's the signal,' she said. 'The festival's over, and the angels can go home now. You didn't finish the route.'

'I finished it yesterday.'

He remembered coming back to the car park and seeing the last angel, this one on the roof of the building across the street: a sombre, life-sized angel brandishing a sword as if he were about to drive the whole city into the ocean. But it was a woman and not a man, the poet had said — he had seen her through his binoculars.

She left the room after the phone rang, but gestured for him to wait. He stared out of the dirty window, watching the distant sky turn red. He looked at the strange clouds, with their black and white stripes. The clouds in Australia really were lined with silver and gold. In just one week, he had inexplicably fallen in love with the country. He had gone there with no expectations, assuming it would be a kind of America. But it had been completely different. The sense of spaciousness and freedom that glowed on every face seemed to find expression in the clouds racing across that vast sky. He longed to follow them into that empty land, into the hot sandy plains he had seen on his maps.

Wistfully he recited to himself the strange names derived from Aboriginal words, as a kind of incantation or promise. Still, he had seen almost no Aboriginal people in Perth. He had told her that, but she had not pursued the matter.

She came back in with two glasses of whisky – no ice, no water – filled to the brim. She drank hers quickly, then the two of them sat together for a while, until they heard a bus honking in the street below.

'It's the angel party!' She laughed. 'Tonight we're being expelled from Paradise! All the angels have been invited to a party at one of the beaches up north.'

'Can I come?'

'Of course. Everyone you saw yesterday along the route will be there, plus the director, the production assistants, the people who organised it, the extras, the whole lot. Including all the angels.'

She had been right. She was greeted with loud cheers, then kissed and hugged by the angel contingent on the bus – men and women in jeans and sweatshirts. He tried to make himself invisible, but he need not have bothered since no one took any notice of him anyway. Someone shoved a glass of beer into his hand; it seemed that the drinking had already begun. Over the shouting he could hear the music of the Bee Gees. A few people were even trying to dance in the bus. The noise was indescribable. When they reached the shore, they found other buses parked there. Lost angels were walking up and down the beach, by themselves or arm in arm. He could still see a rosy glow on the horizon, but later, when he looked again, the moonlight was surfing the high waves. Its gleam kept disappearing under the water and then popping up again. There was an elaborate buffet in the party tent, but he was not hungry. He watched her, occasionally losing sight of her; he watched her dance with wild abandon, first with the angel from the car park, and then with another angel, a man with red hair. From time to time someone shouted something at him, most of which he did not understand. He also caught a glimpse of the Tasmanian poet, twirling drunkenly in the sand with the crop-haired angel, still wearing his snowy white wings. The whip cracks of the music kept getting louder and louder until he could feel the vibrations deep inside him. He tried to get closer to her, but she seemed to be avoiding him. She was constantly surrounded by other angels – young men whose muscular bodies, shaped by a lifetime of jogging and surfing, would not have looked out of place on the ceiling of the Sistine Chapel.

'Hey, Dutchie!' the Dane shouted, and he pushed a girl into his arms. The girl immediately extricated herself, glared at him in a drunken rage and spat on the ground. The Dane started to drag him away, but all of a sudden *she* was there, as if she had been keeping an eye on him all along. They headed out towards the beach. Everywhere he looked, people and angels were lying in the sand. He heard the sound of breaking glass and laughter, and saw the glowing tips of cigarettes. People were laughing, drinking, kissing. He saw a naked angel plunge into the ocean, wings and all, and then he did not see or hear anything except the surf — a steady rise and fall that ended in a silky thump as the oily, gleaming-black, moonlit waves collapsed and went rushing up the beach. There, where the water ended and the land began, she stopped and threw her wings around him. He could not see her face, but he felt her kiss his eyes and run her hand over his face, felt her soft and yet surprisingly hard wings as they held him captive, felt her sink slowly to her knees and then lie on the sand. From far away came the sound of the music in the beach tent. The desire that he had been feeling all this time, from the moment he first saw her — lying curled up on the floor with her feet bare, her face hidden and wearing those wings — now swept over his body, and as he started to undress her, he noticed that she was looking away from him with her eyes wide open, though he could feel her fingernails gently scraping his neck, and at that exact moment, the beach was raked by the revealing white beam of a spotlight. Sirens wailed as police jeeps roared on to the beach from both sides. In the lightning-like flashes he saw angels running in all directions, heard screams and shouts and shrill police whistles, realised that she was saying something to him, though he could not hear what it was above the noise, and then, before he could stop her, she had crouched down on one knee, like a sprinter at the start of a match, dashed off as if propelled from a catapult, raced in and out of the light, and disappeared. As for him, he had walked off, away from the tumult, until he could no longer see or hear a thing, and had simply stayed where he was until dawn. At daybreak, he saw a beach littered with bottles, T-shirts, syringes, condoms, wings. He hitchhiked into town and waited in his hotel for a sign from her until it was time to leave for the airport. But no sign had come.

15

HER HANDS MOVED IN LARGE DESCRIPTIVE CIRCLES OVER his back, then made that familiar gesture — the sign that he was supposed to stand up. But he did not want to stand up, he did not want to stand up ever again. He stood up anyway. Life, he thought, is a stupid invention. She looked at him expectantly with her impish smile.

'Why were you in such a hurry to leave the beach?' he asked.

'I didn't have a work permit. I did not want to be deported.'

'I thought the world was your home.'

She shrugged, then placed her right hand on his left shoulder. 'Do you remember what I said to you then?' she asked.

'No,' he said. 'There was so much noise that I couldn't hear you. What did you say?'

'Angels can't be with people.'

For a moment he was rooted to the spot, then he felt her hand push him gently but firmly towards the door. On his way out, he saw Herr Dr Krüger sitting on a chair, awaiting his turn. Above the man's cheerful greeting, he heard her voice say, 'See you next time, OK?'

But it was too late to respond.

EPILOGUE

'EPILOGUE, from Gr. *epilogos*, conclusion – *epi* and *lego*, to speak. A speech or short poem addressed to the spectators by one of the actors, after the conclusion of a drama.'

From *New Webster Encyclopedic Dictionary of the English Language*, 1952

ANOTHER STATION. LICHTENBERG, BERLIN. I LIKE THINGS that rhyme, even though I myself do not write rhyming poetry. Berlin is the departure point for trains to Poland and Russia. I have an appointment here, though I do not know it yet. The schedule reads: 'Warszawa Centralna 20.55, Minsk 08.49, Smolensk 14.44, Moskva Belorusskaya 20.18.' Different journeys, different trains. I am going on a journey to make up for a loss. Anyone who has ever written a book knows the feeling. A leave-taking of sorts, and therefore always a form of mourning. For a year or two you have lived with your characters, you have given them names that may or may not suit them, you have made them laugh and cry, they have made you laugh and cry, and after that you have sent them on their way, into the big wide world. You hope they will be OK, that they will have enough breath to live for a long, long time. You have left them to their own devices, but it feels as if they have left you. So here you are, alone in a deserted station in what used to be East Berlin. It does not get much sadder than this.

'Wallowing in self-pity won't help,' Almut would say, and that is exactly what I mean. They go on talking to you. They have been talking to each other for two years, and you have been listening. The question is where does it all begin? If the first word came from me, does that mean the second one did too? Last night I jotted down a sentence that I cannot make sense of this morning. My handwriting is always a gauge of how much I have drunk the night before.

Quite a bit, in this case. I can never just say goodbye and let them go. What I scribbled down was this: 'Some voices are clearly written voices.' Or was it 'frightened voices'? I cannot read my own handwriting, but 'written' is better, so let's leave it at that. An announcement is made over the loudspeaker, but my train has not been announced yet. I don't know why I picked Moscow. Probably because I have never been there before. I will not know where I am going, so it will be easier to get lost. Meanwhile, the young man sitting beside me has a cracking whip assailing his ears – a mechanical lash that is repeated over and over again. His head bobs up and down to the beat. He is clearly not someone who has just finished writing a book.

At the end of a project I always have the feeling, for some inexplicable reason, that I am clairvoyant. I mean that literally — not in the sense that I can predict the future, but rather that the things I normally overlook are now seen with great clarity: the fake granite exteriors on the rubbish bins, the yellow-tiled catacombs beneath the station that take you from the U-Bahn to the main station, the corridors that seem to go on forever, the face of the cokehead with the cracking whip next to me. Nothing escapes my notice, but it's of no use to me. It has come too late. The others have already left, they are on their way to Brazil or Australia. In any case I am no longer in control. At the other end of the hall I see two guards in olive-green shirts and white caps — a whiff of the past, a slight shudder. I hear the call of the wild — a three-toned gong — but I still do not see very many people. The train has pulled into the station. Cyrillic letters, curtains, table lamps, everything as it should be. The trains of Dostoyevsky and Nabokov, on their way to Baden-Baden and Biarritz. I do not have to wait long. She is wearing the same outfit she had on in the plane and is carrying the same book — the book I thought I had written, the book I still have not been able to shake off. The last part is true, the first part is not. This time I can read the title right away, as if she has come here specially for me, and perhaps she has. It is the same two words, but in a different order, though in either case Paradise has been lost. Of course we find ourselves in the same compartment. The person who thought that up knew what he was doing. At least this way we'll be able to talk. The conductor's whistle sounds more dramatic here than in other stations. Both of us stare out of the window, perhaps in embarrassment.

I do not know if she's recognised me. During the flight from Friedrichshafen to Berlin she did not look at me once, and as far as I could tell she did not notice me after we landed at Tempelhof either, though you can never be sure. In any case the man who picked her up at the airport is nowhere now in sight.

A couple of fat Russians waddle along the platform, loaded down with so many suitcases they can barely carry them all. As the train glides out of the station, I see that it is raining: a grey city in a grey shroud. In my mind's eye I can see where the now-invisible Wall used to be. Another book that the writer thought was finished, though things are never that simple.

'So what do you think of the book?' I ask. I have never been very clever at striking up conversations with strangers, but in my present mood I am much more daring. Those legs, which were too far away from me on the plane, are now excitingly close. The khaki is stretched over her thighs, showing the powerful muscles underneath. I do not know whether she caught my glance, but she parts her thighs ever so slightly – and that takes my breath away. As I have already explained, for weeks after a project I feel a heightened awareness – a mixture of excitement and longing – which I still have not learned to cope with. Perhaps women are more used to this kind of thing. In any case, she stares out of the window, looking right past me, at the yellowy stubble beside the tracks, the rust-coloured rocks between the sleepers, the city gradually being enveloped by the veil of rain, a pale ship on the horizon.

She has laid the open book on the seat beside her. I can see the old-fashioned spelling of a facsimile edition. My title, but inverted.

'I don't know,' she says. 'It's a rather depressing book. The whole thing seems to be based on a misunderstanding, in which case the punishment is too severe. "Misunderstanding" is such a lovely word, isn't it? What started out as a misunderstanding has gone on to repeat itself over and over again into infinity. You could add a dash of wilful disobedience to that if you want to, though it's usually not necessary. A woman listens to a serpent just once and is cast out for all time, and then a ship lands on an unknown coast where people with painted bodies are hiding in the bushes, or early one evening a woman drives into the wrong neighbourhood and will never be the same again. You know, I think the title is the best part. In that sense the story never really ends. Why do you think writers do that? Do they do it on purpose, so they can have something to write about the next time? Actually, when you get right down to it, I don't know any books that *aren't* about misunderstandings: *Hamlet*, *Madame Bovary*, Marcel who didn't realise that Gilberte loved him, Othello who believed Iago . . . If you stop and think about it —'

Just then, the conductor burst into our compartment to check the tickets, which took forever since the various bits of paper had been stapled together.

'If you stop and think about it?' I asked her, after he had gone.

She laughed, then said, 'Are you sure you want hear what I have to say?'

'Yes,' I said.

'Why? Do you really think it's so important?'

I noticed that her eyes were green, and I also understood that she was seeing me for the first time.

I paused. It was necessary to strike the right tone. I took one last look at the snow-capped Alps in Vorarlberg, at the rock paintings in Ubirr and the Sickness Dreaming Place, at the old man with the signet ring who at that very moment was being laid to rest in Darwin, at the deserted bedroom above the luxurious gardens of Jardins where the *bem-te-vi* sang its high-pitched song, and finally at the only one who was left, and said, 'Because the last sentence is the most important one.'

'And you'd like me to say it?'

I did not answer. I waited.

'Honestly,' she said, 'it's so easy, you could have written it yourself. Have you ever thought about the creator of Paradise – a place where there were no misunderstandings? It must have been incredibly boring. Whoever thought that up must have meant it as a form of punishment. Only a very bad writer could have come up with something like that. Is that good enough for a last sentence?'

'All I have to do now is add a place and a date,' I said.

'And an epilogue,' she said. 'You usually have one, don't you? Here, I've already found you one.' She opened the book to a page towards the back, marked by a slip of paper, and then passed it to me. The lines she wanted me to read had been underlined in pencil.

Amsterdam, February 2003 – Es Consell,
San Luis, 26 August 2004

They looking back, all th' eastern side beheld
Of Paradise, so late thir happie seat,
Wav'd over by that flaming Brand, the Gate
With dreadful Faces throng'd and fierie Armes.
Som natural tears they drop'd, but wip'd them soon;
The World was all before them, where to choose
Thir place of rest, and Providence thir guide:
They hand in hand with wand'ring steps and slow,
Through Eden took thir solitarie way.

Milton, *Paradise Lost*, Book XII